Cross-Dressing Villainess Cecilia Sylvie

4

Hiroro Akizakura

Illustration by **Dangmill**

YEN ON

NEW YORK

Cross-Dressing Villainess Cecilia Sylvie 4

Hiroro Akizakura

TRANSLATION BY KIKI PIATKOWSKA ❀ COVER ART BY DANGMILL

AKUYAKU REIJO, CECILIA SYLVIE WA SHINITAKUNAI
NODE DANSO SURUKOTO NI SHITA. Vol.4
©Hiroro Akizakura 2022
First published in Japan in 2022 by KADOKAWA CORPORATION, Tokyo.
English translation rights arranged with KADOKAWA CORPORATION, Tokyo,
through TUTTLE-MORI AGENCY, INC., Tokyo.

English translation © 2023 by Yen Press, LLC

Yen On
150 West 30th Street, 19th Floor
New York, NY 10001

Visit us at yenpress.com • facebook.com/yenpress • twitter.com/yenpress
yenpress.tumblr.com • instagram.com/yenpress

First Yen On Edition: April 2023
Edited by Yen On Editorial: Maya Deutsch
Designed by Yen Press Design: Liz Parlett

Yen On is an imprint of Yen Press, LLC.
The Yen On name and logo are trademarks of Yen Press, LLC.

The publisher is not responsible for websites (or their content) that are not owned by the publisher.

Library of Congress Cataloging-in-Publication Data
Names: Akizakura, Hiroro, author. | Dangmill, illustrator. | Piatkowska, Kiki, translator.
Title: Cross-dressing villainess Cecilia Sylvie / Hiroro Akizakura ; illustration by Dangmill ;
translation by Kiki Piatkowska.
Other titles: Akuyaku reijo, cecilia sylvie wa shinitakunai. English
Description: First Yen On edition. | New York, NY : Yen On, 2021. | Audience: Ages 13+ |
Summary: Reincarnated as a villainess in a video game, Cecilia avoids her death flag by masquerading
as a man, cross-dressing and assuming a new identity, trying not to let her guise slip with the prince.
Identifiers: LCCN 2021039071 | ISBN 9781975334215 (v. 1 ; trade paperback) |
ISBN 9781975334239 (v. 2 ; trade paperback) | ISBN 9781975342920 (v. 3 ; trade paperback) |
ISBN 9781975363994 (v. 4 ; trade paperback)
Subjects: CYAC: Fantasy. | Male impersonators—Fiction. | Video games—Fiction. |
Secrets—Fiction. | Princes—Fiction. | LCGFT: Fantasy fiction. | Light novels.
Classification: LCC PZ7.1.A3927 Cr 2021 | DDC [Fic]—dc23
LC record available at https://lccn.loc.gov/2021039071

ISBNs: 978-1-9753-6399-4 (paperback)
978-1-9753-6400-7 (ebook)

10 9 8 7 6 5 4 3 2 1

LSC-C

Printed in the United States of America

CONTENTS

Name: Cecilia Sylvie

Gilbert Sylvie

Cecilia's younger adoptive brother and a love interest in the game. Helps her pose as a boy at school.

Oscar Abel Prosper

Crown prince. Cecilia's fianc[e] and a love interest in the gam[e.]

Cecil Admina

Cecilia's male alter ego, the son of a baron. Known as the school prince.

Cecilia Sylvie

Daughter of Duke Sylvie. A villainess who appears in *Holy Maiden of Vleugel Academy 3*.

Cross-Dressing Villainess Cecilia Sylvie

4

Characters

Jade Benjamin

A young merchant. Cecilia's classmate and a love interest in the game.

Lean Rhazaloa

A daughter to a baron. The protagonist of *Holy Maiden of Vleugel Academy 3*.

Elza Hawkins

A cleric serving at the shrine. A big fan of Cecil.

Prince Janis

An enigmatic character encountered as the final boss on many routes of the game.

You could liken my significance to the crown of thorns. To the chalice, spear, and nails. Sometimes, I symbolized the remains of a deity, and other times, I was a monument to one.

You could also draw a comparison to the sacred mirror, sword, and jewels from yet another culture.

I was like a temple, beckoning from the outskirts of a city. Some might liken me to the sky at a time of drought, others to a river during a raging flood.

In other words, I was an object of worship. An integral part of a religion. A passive idol for people to revere.

"I didn't even want to become a Holy Maiden..."

Confined between the walls of the White Shrine, I bemoaned my fate, as I did most days. I wasn't resentful toward anyone in particular. The people around me were all very good, and it was with the best of intentions, out of kindness and consideration, that they kept me there. It was because they venerated me.

Yet it was undeniable that their good intentions, kindness, and consideration had put me in this very frustrating position.

For so many years, decades even, I had been robbed of my freedom. This shrine was my prison, and I could only dream of life outside.

⭢ CHAPTER 1 ⭢ The White Shrine

Vleugel Academy had its very own prince.

He had glossy hair the color of butterscotch and blue eyes you could drown in. His beautifully-shaped lips were always curved up in a smile, the high bridge of his nose gave him a noble look, and his limbs were long and slender.

His bewitchingly androgynous appearance and infinitely graceful movements made him so stunning that he'd easily rival any femme fatale.

And his irresistible sweet-talk, practically ripped from the pages of a storybook, ensured his popularity was unshakable.

This prince was none other than Cecil Admina.

And what was the Vleugel Academy prince, or should we say, the cross-dressing daughter of Duke Sylvie, busy with that day?

"Thank you for your service. You're all working so hard."

"Aaaaaaaah! It's Prince Cecil!"

He was casting his princely charm about as usual, only this time it was on the premises of the White Shrine, where the Holy Maiden resided.

"Honestly, can't you tone it down a little, Cecil? It's the shrine, for goddess' sake."

"Heh-heh… It was just a greeting. I didn't say anything inappropriate."

Cecilia smiled awkwardly and scratched her cheek when Oscar gave her the stink eye as they walked down the hallway.

Shortly after Advent—in the middle of November, to be more precise—Cecilia and her friends received a summons from the Holy Maiden. And so they traveled to Torche, the bastion of the Caritade faith. Although it was located within the Kingdom of Prosper, the city-state was governed by the Church of Caritade with the Holy Maiden as its head. Its citizens were all members of the clergy, nuns, or monks, but Torche was in no way isolated from the rest of the kingdom. There was no physical border around the small city, and considering that pilgrims and pious worshippers arrived there in droves every day, it would been impractical to have one.

As for why Cecil and company had been summoned to the White Shrine…

"This Holy Maiden must be a very conscientious person, inviting us over to thank us for our courageous actions on Advent Day!" Jade, walking in front, was all enthusiasm.

The Maiden wished to see the heroes who'd prevented carnage on that fateful festival day. That was why Gilbert, who wasn't considered one of the knights, Huey, who didn't officially have anything to do with the Holy Maiden, and Grace, who'd helped Mordred tend to the wounded, were included in the invitation.

Still feeling guilty about what happened, Eins and Zwei had excused themselves. Mordred also turned the invitation down, insisting that he couldn't possibly leave his sick sister alone for several days, and Grace decided not to attend as well. That left seven of them: Cecilia, Lean, Gilbert, Oscar, Jade, Dante, and Huey.

"Aren't you barking up the wrong tree, Your Highness? If anyone was behaving inappropriately, it was the nuns, getting all worked up just because a boy spoke to them," commented Gilbert, frowning at the animated squeals of the nuns they'd left behind.

His gripe didn't go unnoticed by their guide. Elza Hawkins, as that was her name, was the abbess in charge of all the nuns serving at the shrine. Despite being a woman of the cloth, she was around the same age as Cecilia and her friends. She wore her ginger hair in braids, had freckles on her cheeks, and sported glasses. She turned back around to them.

"Those girls have yet to become full-fledged nuns, so the vows they've taken aren't as strict the ones for full-fledged members of the clergy. There are no rules prohibiting displays of excitement."

"What vows?" asked Huey, tilting his neck.

Jade was the one to answer.

"Nuns and monks take three vows—chastity, poverty, and obedience."

"Huh. I guess some people are into that kind of life. Sounds like a big commitment."

"Heh-heh, it doesn't appeal to you, does it?"

"Not really..."

Elza looked at them with a little smile playing on her lips.

"Besides, Lord Cecil gets special treatment here."

"What sort of special treatment?" asked Cecilia.

"In my convent, it's perfectly acceptable to be bowled over by you," Elza replied with longing in her voice.

Cecilia responded with a blank stare of confusion. Elza stopped and turned back toward them, bringing her hands to her cheeks, which had taken on a rosy tinge.

"You see, ever since Advent Day, everyone at the shrine has been whispering that Lord Cecil might be a transmigration of Ian..."

"Ian, as in Ian Bruel? The man who rescued the goddess and laid the foundations of our kingdom?!"

The goddess was the central figure in the kingdom's origin myth, but the tale had another central figure—the prince of a demon-infested land, who accompanied the goddess in her battles through thick and thin. He went on to become the goddess' beloved and formed new nation with her, naming it the Kingdom of Prosper in hopes that it would flourish.

"That's Oscar's ancestor you're talking about!" exclaimed Jade.

"According to the legend," Oscar clarified flatly.

Cecilia widened her eyes and pointed to herself in disbelief.

"You really think I'm that hero?!"

"I do!"

Elza's tranquil expression vanished as her eyes glinted in pure adoration. She clasped her hands together, looking for all the world like a young girl in love.

"I heard that your rescue of Lady Lean was so magnificent, it was like watching the events from the legend unfold in front of one's own eyes! Lo and behold, you appeared in the ring of fire, cradled Lady Lean, and carried her to safety! Some have even gone as far as to say they glimpsed feathered wings momentarily appearing on your back when you jumped down with the maiden in your arms!"

She should really take people's stories with a grain of salt...,

Cecilia thought, smiling wryly as the abbess gave them her impassioned speech.

In Elza's secondhand account of the events, Lord Cecil had rescued Lean before he mowed down a swarm of enemies, the last of which was a giant, whom he defeated in a heart-stopping duel. And this was no ordinary giant, mind you—he was so powerful he could pierce the heavens, shatter mountains, and split the sea in half—which made Cecil's victory all the more incredible.

So this is how legends get started...

The story had grown as it spread. It got bigger and bigger, taking on a life of its own. It didn't have much in common with the actual facts at this point. The embellishments had obscured the truth, like a pearl being formed around a grain of sand.

Elza cleared her throat and apologized upon completing the story, realizing that she'd been in a world of her own to the consternation of her companions. Her cheeks were still flushed as she went back to the original topic.

"So, um, it all boils down to the fact that the news of Lord Cecil's heroic deeds convinced us that he's Ian reborn. Needless to say, our religion does not prohibit us from venerating Ian. On the contrary, admiring him is a laudable act of faith. This is why I said earlier that being infatuated with Lord Cecil is permitted here."

"Good for you, Cecil. Next thing you know, you'll be a god," Lean whispered into Cecilia's ear.

"I don't like this at all!"

And she meant it. All this recognition negated the painstaking efforts she'd taken to disguise herself as a boy. Her goal was to avoid the spotlight, stay out of trouble, and be nothing more than a forgettable background character in the game's story—at least that had been her plan to begin with.

Not that I can avoid drawing attention at this point. Or not get involved...

But she didn't want to be treated as a god. Or a transmigration of one, or whatever.

"Now that you know how things are, be warned, Lord Cecil. You must be on your guard!"

"Against what...?"

"I cannot vouch that there won't be any nuns who might pursue you with fierce tenacity, believing you to be Ian!"

"P-pursue me...?"

"Also, in the event something happened between you and my flock, I'm not even certain if I would be in a position to punish them. Whether you are a transmigration of Ian or not is pure speculation at the moment, but the upper clergy is nonetheless divided over if getting involved with you would constitute a breach of the vow of chastity or could be seen as serving our god with both body and soul."

Cecilia found this warning very disturbing and struggled to keep a straight face. She might have made a huge mistake coming to the shrine. But how could she have guessed that this holy place was filled with devilishly horny nuns?

"You would do well not to eat or drink anything offered to you by anyone other than myself, lest you discover that it's been laced with sleeping agents...or worse."

"Or worse?"

"It's best not to ask for peace of mind," Elza replied with her sweetest smile yet.

Cecilia shivered as a chill ran down her spine.

"I don't mean it in an insulting way, of course, but it might be helpful to you to think of the nuns as a pack of hungry wolves and their squeals of excitement as hunting howls when they sight their prey. Oh, and here we are!"

Elza stopped in front of a door and turned toward them with a smile, putting her hand on the door handle.

"Please wait outside. I'll call you when the Holy Maiden is ready to see you."

The audience hall they were let into was simply gorgeous, framed by white walls decorated with gold leaf, large windows in the shape of multi-pointed stars, and paintings of scenes from the legend from floor to ceiling. It could easily pass for a chamber in an aristocratic mansion.

"I thought the headquarters of the Church of Caritade would have a more austere atmosphere. Elza's convivial attitude also surprised me. It goes to show you should never make assumptions," Jade remarked offhandedly, plopping down on a sofa and craning his neck this way and that, taking it all in with interest.

Cecilia followed suit, sitting down next to him.

"Yeah. I also didn't think the shrine would be this opulent!"

"The nuns take a vow of poverty, so I thought they'd be living in much simpler quarters!"

The shrine looked magnificent even from the outside, and it wasn't only because of its sheer size. Its architecture also elicited gasps.

The round pillars out front were pleasingly symmetrical, while the building's monumental onion-shaped dome awed visitors. Near the entrance stood a statue of the goddess, carved with such minute detail it was truly lifelike.

Cecilia and her friends had been stupefied by the splendor when they'd disembarked from the carriage. The shrine, together with the other facilities on its grounds, might even have given the royal palace a run for its money.

"This place is the symbol of the faith, meant to inspire awe in everyone who sees it. And what better way to display the power of your influence than erect a grand building with the money from donations?" Gilbert supplied an explanation.

Girls from noble houses or wealthy merchant families would also sometimes be sent to spend time at the shrine to practice virtues such as modesty. The amount of money their families would donate on these occasions, though, was far from modest—it constituted a small fortune. Enough to pay for the construction of a fine new mansion, in some cases.

"The Church has a keen business sense to make their headquarters a tourist attraction in addition to a religious destination," Jade observed with a smile, his voice bouncy with enthusiasm.

Cecilia, who'd been anxious about the trip, found his cheeriness puzzling.

"You sure are stoked today, Jade. You've been on fire since we got in the carriage."

"Um, yeah? What's so strange about that? Aren't you excited? The Holy Maiden's going to thank us in person for being amazing! If that's not a reason to be happy, I don't know what is! And it's also fun to be on a trip together again!" He looked deep into Cecil's eyes and added, "It's great to have you with us this time around!"

"Huh?"

"You weren't there when we were visiting the Sylvies. I was so disappointed."

"Oh, sorry…"

She felt a pang of guilt. Jade was referring to the time when her friends had shown up unannounced for a sleepover at her family residence. She WAS there, but not under the guise of Cecil, so Jade hadn't recognized her. It made her feel sorry for him to know he had missed her company.

"I was going to find out your contact details through the traders' guild to invite you along, but Gil wouldn't let me."

"Really?"

"He said I shouldn't pressure you to join us, since you were probably busy. Oscar agreed with him, so I let it go."

"I didn't know…," muttered Cecilia, her face pale.

She'd been *this* close to being found out, and she hadn't even been aware. Boy, was she glad that Gilbert was on the ball and averted disaster.

Jade clasped Cecilia's hand, completely oblivious to how he'd rattled her.

"Let's make up for last time and pack in as much fun as we can! We're free to go sightseeing tomorrow, right?"

"Uh-huh. That'll be fun," Cecilia replied, not managing to match Jade's level of enthusiasm.

They would be staying at the shrine for three days and two nights. The trip from the capital took half a day by horse-drawn carriage. They'd departed before first light, so it was still only afternoon, but going back the next day would have been unnecessarily exhausting, both for them and the horses. That's why they'd extended their stay, reserving the second day for resting up after the journey. They'd be free to do whatever they liked then.

"We definitely have to check out the Temple of Marine! And the nearby Laugier Chapel. I read there's even an art gallery!"

"It sounds like there's a lot to see."

"Yes! We won't be bored!"

Jade was so excited, you'd think he was going on a school trip. Cecilia slowly exhaled, staring at the ceiling.

"Hmm, you're selling me on this excursion, Jade. Maybe it will be fun after all."

"Sure will! And did you know they've got a huge bathhouse here? You can share a hot tub with me!"

"What?!" Oscar interjected out of the blue.

Jade misinterpreted his reaction.

"Want to join us for a soak in a luxuriously large hot tub? Just like on the field trip! Or is that nothing special to you? But, but, helping each other wash off soap before jumping into the tub is something I've, like, always wanted to do! Maybe I idealized it in my head because I don't have any siblings and always bathe alone, but I totally want to do this!"

"Jade, listen, I don't really—" Cecilia tried to get a word in, but Jade steamrolled over her.

"I'll wash soap off your back, Oscar, Cecil will do mine, and you'll do Cecil's!"

"Absolutely not!" bellowed Oscar, his cheeks turning scarlet.

At that exact moment the door opened, and Elza announced: "The Holy Maiden is ready to receive you."

Their audience with the Holy Maiden was over in five minutes. They didn't actually see, nor speak with the maiden—she sat hidden behind a bamboo blind and communicated with them by writing letters on parchment, which Elza read aloud to them. They got a glimpse of the Holy Maiden's silhouette, but that was it.

It went without saying that they were pretty disappointed, especially in the light of the fact that they'd spent half the day on the road just for this.

I wanted to at least see what the Holy Maiden looked like..., Cecilia thought to herself as she began unpacking in her allocated room.

She made sure to get a single room this time, so as not to repeat the nerve-racking experience of sharing lodgings with someone who might find out her secret. The shrine actually had plenty of guest rooms available. They must have gotten a regular stream of overnight visitors.

I didn't think anything of the Holy Maiden not making an appearance at the Advent Festival because that's how it is in the game, too, but now I'm wondering if there's a reason why she won't let anyone see her face...

Lean had taken over the Holy Maiden's duties last Advent, but it was certainly the Holy Maiden herself who'd led the celebrations a year before that. Something was smelling fishy.

Cecilia was laying out her changes of clothes, a sense of unease nagging at her, when someone knocked on her door.

"Just a moment!"

She thought it might be Gilbert, but it wasn't him.

"Lord Cecil, may I come in?"

"Huh? Lean?!"

Cecilia was so surprised her voice came out more high-pitched than she'd intended. She rushed to open the door. Lean smiled and entered the room before Cecilia could stop her. She closed the door behind her and turned the key in the lock.

"Is something wrong, Lean? What happened?"

"Nothing happened. I came to talk to you about our strategy."

"Strategy? For what?"

Lean had dropped her fake persona and was back to her usual bossy self.

"You won't get far on your own, so I'm kindly offering my help."

"Er... Sorry, but I have no idea what you're talking about?"

Lean frowned at her confused friend.

"Are you joking? Don't tell me you've forgotten your objective!"

"Wait... Aah, so that's what you meant!"

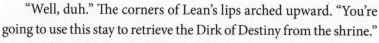

"Well, duh." The corners of Lean's lips arched upward. "You're going to use this stay to retrieve the Dirk of Destiny from the shrine."

Cecilia nodded with determination.

According to Grace, the Dirk of Destiny was required to put an end to the appearance of Obstructions once and for all. Cecilia had needed to befriend both Eins and Zwei in order to trigger the True Love route, which was the only branch of the game where you could access the dagger.

"So the way it works is, the Holy Maiden or a Holy Maiden candidate has to thrust the dirk into the altar at the heart of the shrine to banish Obstructions from this world?"

"That's right."

Grace had told Cecilia that the knife was hidden somewhere underground beneath the shrine. Its existence was only spoken of in whispers, even here at the shrine, and no one had ever seen it or knew of its precise location.

In the game, a series of coincidences leads the heroine to wander into the room where the Dirk of Destiny is concealed, which is how she manages to obtain it. Mordred, who has been researching Obstructions, reveals its significance to the player.

"And how are you going to find it?"

"Grace gave me instructions."

Cecilia produced a folded sheet of paper with directions on it from her pocket. Lean took it from her, tracing her finger along her lower lip, as if in deep thought.

"These directions are quite vague."

"I'm glad she could remember even this much from her past life. Especially when you consider the game's genre."

As was common with dating sims for girls, *Holy Maiden of Vleugel Academy 3* was a visual novel. In game, locations are presented as static backgrounds, with images of the characters and a dialogue box overlaid on top of them. Grace must have paid incredible attention to detail to figure out how to get to the dagger based on those backgrounds alone.

"I see she told you what landmarks to look out for, but I still think we'll need to gather some more information."

"You'll help me find the dagger?" Cecilia asked in an uncertain tone of voice.

Lean nodded firmly.

"I will. Not that I'm excited for it, but I owe you for saving my life. I don't like to harbor any debts. So if I do happen to become indebted to someone, I make sure to repay them as soon as possible. You should know that about me."

Cecilia wouldn't have guessed that Lean felt indebted to her. In fact, her perspective on Advent Day was different; the way Cecilia saw things, *she* had endangered Lean by getting caught up in a crisis of her own making that had taken her friend away from the ceremony.

"Also, this is going to be a risky operation. There's so much at stake that I simply can't leave it all to you. Don't try to stop me, 'cause I won't listen. I'm helping you, and that's final!"

"But…"

"What? You think I'll just get in the way?"

Cecilia shook her head.

"No, but you said it yourself—it's going to be dangerous. Who knows what the nuns might do to us if they find out what we're up to…"

They've been talking about "retrieving" the Dirk of Destiny, but it would be more accurate to call what they were doing "stealing." Even though the nuns didn't know for a fact that the dagger existed, it belonged to the shrine, and its protectors would assuredly take a dim view of someone taking it away without permission.

"Well, it's only going to be RISKIER if you don't have anyone serving as a lookout or decoy."

"You're not wrong, but…" Cecilia was still balking at the idea.

Lean held up her left hand.

"If you really want me not to get involved, fine, but then I won't be giving this to you."

"Wait a minute!"

"I thought Jade's Artifact might come in handy in this situation."

On Lean's wrist was a shiny bracelet with a sparkly green gemstone. Jade's Artifact had the power of stealth. It could grant its wearer a cloak of invisibility, making them undetectable. It was just the item you'd want when going sacred dagger-stealing in a shrine. But why did Lean have it?

"How did you get it from Jade? You didn't tell him about the dirk, did you?!"

"Don't be silly."

"Then how?"

"I asked him if I could borrow it, with the caveat that I couldn't tell him what it was for. That was fine with him."

"Seriously?"

Cecilia reeled, shocked at how easy it had been for Lean to get what she wanted. This bracelet would help immensely…but she wanted to yell at Jade for giving away something so valuable without a second thought.

Seeing that had Cecilia lost the will to fight her after seeing the bracelet, Lean smiled triumphantly.

"That's settled then, isn't it? We'll strike tomorrow after

nightfall. Oh, and I'm not letting you hit the hay tonight until we devise a plan that can cover all eventualities!"

"...Thanks, Lean."

"It's my pleasure."

Lean beamed unreservedly, showing her teeth.

"All together, on three! One, two...three!"

"Prince Ceeeciiil!"

Cecilia forced a smile and raised her right hand in a greeting as the nuns shouted her alter ego's name. It was the day after the audience with the Holy Maiden. Cecilia and her friends were standing outside of the shrine. Blushing nuns were staring at her through the windows, waving. Jade's eyes went from the squeeing girls back to Cecilia.

"They really don't have to hold back when it comes to you, huh."

"Ha-ha..."

"They haven't tried to do anything inappropriate to you, have they?" Gilbert asked with concern.

Cecilia shook her head.

"No, they haven't bothered me in any way. But they've been bringing me, um...offerings, I guess."

"Like what?"

"They've been leaving bunches of flowers, fruit, and foods they cooked outside my door, that sort of thing. Elza noticed and told me they were offerings for me."

"You're getting worshipped in the religious sense now, too, huh," remarked Huey with pity.

"Ha-ha... Yeah..."

Cecilia looked away, embarrassed. It was nice to be admired, but the amount and intensity of attention she was getting here was a massive overdose, and she was at a loss as to how she should respond.

"So there was food among the offerings? I hope you haven't eaten any of it?" Oscar was alarmed after the warning from Elza.

Cecilia shook her head again.

"Not one bite. At first, I thought it would be shame to just throw what they made for me away, but on closer inspection of one cake, for example, I saw all these hairs sticking out of it? That put me off trying anything."

"Eww…"

"You get the sense that these nuns have been bottling up their desires for too long, and now the bottle has shattered…"

Oscar and Huey were seriously taken aback, but Dante just laughed.

"They're only human. It's not healthy to suppress your true nature!"

Jade, meanwhile, found the gross display of putting hair in food concerning.

"You're not really safe here, Cecil. I think you should make sure that you've got one of us with you until we leave this city. I'm really worried something will happen to you if you go out alone. There are a lot of sites to hit, so our group might split up based on who wants to see what, but you should pick someone to accompany you."

"Yeah, maybe…"

As she wondered who to tag along with, her eyes met Gilbert's for a second. He used to be her go-to friend to take along on occasions like this, and everyone was probably thinking she'd invite him this time, too.

"Better to be safe than sorry, huh. I guess I'll stick with you, Jade!"

"What? You want to go with me?"

Jade pointed at himself. Gilbert, standing behind him, seemed a bit thrown off.

"That's an unusual pairing."

"Have you had a falling-out with Gil?" asked Huey, looking from one to the other, trying to read their faces.

Flustered, Cecilia shook her head vigorously.

"No, no, everything's fine between us! It's just that Jade seems to know a lot about Torche, so I thought I might enjoy it more if he showed me around, sharing some trivia."

"You'd like me to be your guide?" Jade blinked.

"Yes, please!"

"Okay, I'm up for that! Let's pair up for today!"

Cecilia could see that Gilbert was looking at her with one eyebrow raised from behind Jade, but she pretended not to notice.

Jade and Cecilia went to see the Temple of Marine and Laugier Chapel first, then headed to a gallery of paintings and other artwork donated by believers. As Jade had explained the previous day, the city was open not only to pilgrims, but to tourists of any kind, so the central plaza was packed tight with stores and food stalls. It was a popular destination for merchants catering to Caritade followers, and Jade had some friends who did their business there.

The art gallery was very impressive indeed. There was no shortage of beautiful objects and paintings on display, presumably donated by wealthy aristocrats whose daughters stayed at the shrine. Tourists and pilgrims milled about, admiring the pieces.

Cecilia kept sighing "Ooh!" and "Aah!" as they walked around the round central plaza and the main streets connecting to it.

"This is a textbook tourist trap!"

"You're right. Unlike the shrine and church grounds, which clearly serve religious purposes and are only partially accessible to visitors, this part of the city appears to have been designed with tourists in mind," elaborated Gilbert.

"Look, there are even souvenir shops!" added Lean.

"I presume the Church doesn't have a stake in these businesses but tolerates them since they benefit the city's economy."

Religion and business weren't terms you'd usually hear together, but here in Torche, they struck the perfect balance. Together, those two forces kept the country running.

Just then, they heard Dante shout. "Gil! Oscar! Come over here for a moment!"

The four of them turned to see Dante beckoning them to come back to a souvenir store they had passed. Huey and Jade were next to him.

Not knowing what Dante might want from them, Gilbert and Oscar were in no hurry to walk over, so Jade ran over to them excitedly and tugged their hands.

"Is there trouble?"

"No, but you won't believe it! Dante found figurines that look just like you two!"

"What…?"

"Just come and see them!" Beaming, Jade started pulling his baffled friends toward the stall.

"Let go!"

"You're pulling my arm off!"

Despite their protests, Gilbert and Oscar followed rather meekly. They both had a soft spot for Jade. His amicable nature was certainly working to his benefit.

Cecilia and Lean stayed behind.

"Everyone's enjoying the trip."

"Looks like it."

Gilbert grimaced when Dante shoved the figurine in his face. Dante laughed as he spoke to them, while Oscar glared angrily. Huey sighed at the others' silliness, resisting as Jade pulled on his arm to get his attention.

Cecilia couldn't help smiling at her friends' antics.

"Oh, by the way…" Lean suddenly remembered something. "I asked the nuns if they'd heard about the Dirk of Destiny or if the shrine has an underground area."

"And? What did they say?" Cecilia lowered her voice to a conspiratorial whisper and leaned in toward Lean, only to find out she'd gotten her hopes up in vain.

"They confirmed that they'd heard about it. But that's it, I'm afraid."

"What a letdown. I tried wringing some info out of Elza, too, but she said the same. Oh, but she at least told me where to find the Mural of Ian! And the grandfather clock that's the other clue!"

"Hmm, that's not much, but I suppose it gives us a chance of finding the dagger…" Lean didn't sound hopeful.

"It's not much to go on, is it…" Cecilia also began to lose spirit.

Lean held her gaze on Cecilia for a few moments before suddenly giving her a rather powerful pat on the back.

"Ow!"

"We'll figure something out, so chin up!"

"Lean…"

"It can't go wrong with me on your side!"

Lean, as confident as ever, pointed at herself elegantly with an open hand and puffed out her chest.

"What we should be doing right now is having a fun day out in town! It's counterproductive to get anxious. We've drawn up a plan, and we're going through with it."

Jade called them over right as Lean finished her pep talk. The girls looked at each other and exchanged smiles.

"Shall we join them?"

"Yes, let's!"

They turned toward the boys and started walking side by side.

A few hours later...

"I'm beat!"

It was evening. Back in her room, Cecilia lay supine on her bed. She couldn't feel her feet from all the walking she'd done, and the large dinner they had after coming back to the shrine made her very sleepy. Her whole body felt leaden, and she feared that if she closed her eyes for longer than a moment, it would be morning the next time she opened them. It was too dangerous to stay in bed, so she jumped off and shook her head.

"Wake up, Cecilia! You've got a special mission tonight! The whole trip will be for nothing if I nod off now!"

Through her efforts, she'd managed to befriend Eins and Zwei. Advent Day had been a nightmare, but it ended with her becoming a hero. All of that had been for this mission—the retrieval of the Dirk of Destiny. She couldn't afford to ruin it by falling asleep.

"But I still have so much time to kill..."

Lean and Cecilia had agreed to begin their stealth operation at midnight. It would be easier for them to explore the shrine when most of its residents were asleep. Plus, in the game, the heroine also finds the dagger in the dead of night. The girls hoped that if they partially matched the game events, luck might just turn out to be on their side.

"I guess I could take a shower now!"

That ought to wake her up. Cecilia went to the en-suite shower room to get the water running...but nothing came out of the shower head.

"Huh?"

She twisted the taps all the way open, but not a drop came out. Was the boiler not working? No, if the boiler had a problem, then there would at least be cold water in the tap.

Cecilia went to find Elza to notify her that there was no water.

"What? It should be running," the abbess said, puzzled. "Let me check your shower. Please wait outside."

Elza smiled and went inside, leaving Cecilia in the hallway. She returned a few minutes later.

"I'm terribly sorry!" She bowed low in apology.

"Um, it's okay, it's not your fault..."

"I'm responsible for hosting you and your friends and ensuring you have a comfortable stay, yet I have failed to do so!"

Elza kept bowing abjectly despite Cecilia's reassurances that she didn't need to apologize. There were tears in her eyes, and her face had drained of color, as if she was afraid Cecilia was going to angrily reprimand her.

There seemed to be a problem with the water pipes. Not only was Elza unable to fix it, she couldn't even pinpoint what was wrong. This was clearly a job for a plumber, but the earliest they could get one to come in was the following day.

"I'm so sorry for the inconvenience, but could you use the communal bathhouse instead?"

"Uh... The bathhouse...?"

"Oh. Do you dislike communal bathing?"

"It's not that I dislike it..."

There was no way she could go to the bathhouse. Reckless as she was, Cecilia was well aware of the risks. There was no guarantee that she'd be alone in there, or that nobody would come in while she was in the middle of cleaning herself. And if someone saw her naked…well.

Seeing Cecilia so discomfited brought fresh tears to Elza's eyes.

"I would let you use a shower in another guest room, but we haven't been having many overnight visitors lately, so the spare rooms aren't currently in a presentable condition. I would have to go wake up one of the nuns and ask her to clean another room for you…"

That would make Cecilia feel really guilty. She'd rather pass. The nuns began their work at dawn every day and went to sleep as soon as the sun set. While it was still early by Cecilia's standards, she didn't have the heart to have Elza rouse one of the tired women for an impromptu room clean. Also, if the other guest rooms were as ridiculously large as the one Cecilia was staying in now, it would probably take hours to clean.

"Should I go and—"

"No, no! Don't worry, I'll manage! Please raise your head!" Cecilia put her hands on Elza's shoulders. The cleric looked up and Cecilia smiled at her warmly. "You have nothing to apologize for!"

"But…looking after you is my duty, entrusted to me by the Holy Maiden…"

Elza still seemed dejected. Cecilia thought for a moment, then reached into her pocket. When she brought out her hand, her fingers were tightly closed around something.

"Give me your palm, Elza."

"Oh? You mean, like this?"

She held out her hand. Cecilia opened her fist and dropped… three pieces of candy onto Elza's palm. They were very cute, wrapped in colorful paper tied with little ribbons on both ends.

Elza opened her eyes wide.

"Why are you giving me these?"

"Jade bought loads when we were out today and handed me a bunch. I couldn't manage to finish them all."

As she explained, Cecilia picked up one of the candies from Elza's hand and unwrapped it to reveal an amber-colored sweet. She held it between two fingers and brought it to Elza's mouth.

"Try it."

A look of confusion passed over Elza's face, but she gave in to Cecilia and reluctantly opened her mouth. Cecilia popped the candy in. Elza covered her mouth with her hand, shocked by the taste.

"It's so sweet!"

"It's candy, of course it's sweet. Oh, do you mean that it's too sweet for you? It's not a very refined treat, I admit..."

Worried, Cecilia peered searchingly into Elza's eyes. The abbess smiled and shook her head.

"It's not too sweet, but it's a bit of a shock for me, since I haven't had anything like this in a long time..."

"So you like hard candy?"

"Yes."

"Then I made the right call!"

Cecilia laughed. Elza squinted as if witnessing a sight too dazzling for her eyes.

"You're always working so hard, Elza. I think you deserve a treat!"

"Thank you, that's very kind..."

Even though she still seemed somewhat embarrassed, the abbess accepted the candy with a happy smile.

"Now what do I do?"

Alone in her room, Cecilia held her head in her hands, despairing over not being able to use the shower. The situation was quite frustrating, since she'd been looking forward to washing off the sweat she worked up from sightseeing the whole day. It felt icky under her wig and the sash wrapped around her chest. What could be the most crucial moment of her life was about to begin, and she'd wanted to prepare for it. She didn't need an elaborate bath, but a quick wash to leave her feeling fresh and ready would have been nice.

"I'll have to ask Lean to let me shower in her room."

Cecilia could count on her friend, surely. A female friend who knew her secret. No problem there. It wouldn't even matter if Lean caught a glimpse of her naked.

Her mind made up, Cecilia picked up a towel and a change of clothes and headed over to Lean's room. She knocked on the door twice.

"Lean, are you there?"

The door opened almost immediately. But it wasn't Lean who opened it.

"H-Huey?!"

It was Lean's boyfriend. Cecilia inwardly cursed her bad timing, her face turning pale. Lean appeared behind Huey.

"Oh, it's Lord Cecil? Can I help you with something?"

"No, um…"

"Why've you got a change of clothes with you?"

"It—it's not what you're thinking!"

She pointlessly tried to hide the bundle of clothing behind her back. She was still dressed as Cecil. The way Huey saw it, she was a dude suddenly visiting his girlfriend at night, bringing a change of clothes… An unwelcome sight, to grossly understate the situation. He was bound to be see her as a threat.

He's…he's going to kill me!

As a former member of the assassin organization Heimat, Huey could probably end her as easily as he could a fly. And he was giving her quite the stare. She had to wriggle out of this somehow.

"S-sorry! Wrong room!"

"Wrong room? I don't think so. You were asking for Lean when you came knocking."

"Wh-what? N-no, you must have misheard!"

"Really?"

"I d-definitely didn't say 'Lean'! It was… It was… Mee-aan!"

"What's that even supposed to be?"

"A meow?"

"Are you kidding me…?"

Huey frowned. Of course he wasn't buying it. Even Cecilia was aware of how nonsensical her defense sounded. Beads of cold sweat started rolling down her cheeks.

W-was Huey this scary in the game too?!

Not that he was glaring at her, but he was obviously wary, suspecting she was up to no good. Lean, standing behind him, seemed quite baffled as well. Cecilia had no other choice but leave it at that and get out of there. Huey might question her about this the next day, but that was something for her future self to worry about.

You'll think of something, tomorrow's Cecilia!

Hoping that she would work something out later, Cecilia turned on her heel as though she was about to start running like her life depended on it. Which was a fair assumption, really…

"What are you doing here, Cecil?"

"Gil?!"

Just then, her brother happened to pass by. He stopped and sized up Cecilia, Huey and Lean, and the bundle of clothes Cecilia was clutching behind her back. He raised an eyebrow. Then he grabbed Cecilia by her wrist.

"I was looking for you everywhere, sheesh!"

"You were?!"

"In retrospect, I shouldn't have asked you to come to my room knowing how you have absolutely no sense of direction."

"Wait, are you saying—"

"Please excuse us."

Gilbert nodded to Lean and Huey, then led Cecilia away by the arm. Huey was still trying to get a word in, but her brother was walking so fast that she didn't even get to turn back to take one last look at him.

A few minutes later, when they could no longer be seen from Lean's room, Gilbert finally let go of Cecilia's hand. She hung her head.

"Thanks so much, Gilbert. I don't know what I'd have done without you!"

"What was that about anyway?"

"I just wanted to ask Lean if she'd let me use her shower because mine's broken. I didn't think Huey would be there…"

The explanation wiped the annoyed frown off his face. Cecilia had done nothing wrong. She was still crestfallen, though.

"I can't go to the communal bath. I guess I'll have to make do without a shower today."

The unplanned encounter with Huey had sent her heart rate through the roof, so she no longer needed to bathe to wake herself up. She'd have to put up with feeling clammy and worn-out that night.

Gilbert observed Cecilia for a moment, rubbing his chin. She must have made for quite the pitiful sight. After a brief moment of contemplation, he dropped a bomb on her with a well-meaning suggestion.

"You could use the shower in my room."

"What?"

It felt as though time had frozen for a second.

One hour later...

"Thanks for letting me use the shower, Gil. Sorry to be such a bother," Cecilia apologized sincerely, wringing her hair out and drying it with a towel.

"It was no trouble at all," replied Gilbert from the sofa, not even lifting his eyes from the book he was reading. "This was the only viable option."

"Ha-ha..."

"Besides, I'm sure you'd get yourself into an even bigger mess if I hadn't invited you over."

"What do you mean?" Cecilia tilted her head.

Gilbert finally looked up at her.

"Wouldn't you have ended up taking your chances and going to the communal bath on the sly?"

"No, that's too risky..."

"When you try to put up with something making you uncomfortable, your resolve melts quicker than an ice cream on a hot summer day. Your chain of thought would be: 'As long as I'm the only person in the bath, my secret will be safe!' And then, 'I'll be totally fine if I wait until after everyone's gone to sleep!' Tell me I'm wrong."

"That does sound like me..."

"See?"

Cecilia was astonished at how Gilbert could predict exactly how she would have acted. Perhaps he understood her better than she did herself.

"You're so oblivious to danger that you'd waltz right into a den of lions. Fortunately, some lions have self-restraint."

"Wait, I'm lost. What lions are you talking about?"

"Never mind," Gilbert said curtly and sighed. Then he muttered, "You can be ignorant to people's feelings toward you."

Cecilia tilted her head slightly, finding Gilbert's remarks rather enigmatic.

"Well, anyway. You saved me today! Thanks, Gil!"

She smiled at him with gratitude and trust. Gilbert noticed that and widened his eyes for a moment, but then he focused on his book again. Were his ears a little flushed, or was it just the light playing tricks? Cecilia couldn't see his eyes very well beneath his bangs, but she could have sworn they were a bit red around the edges.

Forgetting those details almost the same moment she noticed them, Cecilia sat down on the sofa next to Gilbert. And left a gap between them. Normally they'd be sitting so close they'd be touching, or even leisurely leaning against each other, but not this time. Gilbert looked at the space and then at Cecilia.

"I actually have another thing to thank you for, which I only just found out about. The guys' summer vacation trip to our house."

"Ah, that."

"I'd like to repay you for all those favors somehow, but I don't know what you'd like!"

"You don't know what I'd like?"

After a few seconds' pause, Gilbert closed his book and put it on the coffee table in front of the sofa.

"How about you let me hold you?" he said, his tone far different than usual.

"...Huh?"

Cecilia wasn't sure how to take that. She edged a bit farther away from him.

"What's the matter? You used to hug me all the time, even when I asked you not to. It shouldn't be a big deal to you."

"Um, well..."

Theoretically, it shouldn't have been a big deal but... Her forehead started glistening with perspiration in spite of the fact she'd just taken a shower. She was suddenly feeling very hot, and she suspected that her face had gone red.

"I miss physical contact with you, Cecilia. I haven't been getting much of that lately."

"Y-you want me to touch you more...?"

"I was just teasing you." Gilbert huffed out a laugh. "But it's true that you've been giving me a wide berth. I noticed you were steering clear of both me and Oscar today."

"Ha-ha..." Cecilia gave an awkward chuckle.

She couldn't deny it. And she hadn't done that unconsciously, either—she was intentionally keeping her distance from the two men to avoid getting their hopes up while she was still working out whether she had feelings for them. She figured that was the right thing to do.

Gilbert could read her like an open book, though. Always one step ahead of her, he made her feel as if she were the younger sibling.

"Just so you know, it stings both of us."

"Huh?"

"Oscar's feeling alienated, and it makes me sad that you're giving me the cold shoulder."

"I'm sorry it upsets you..."

"I'm not trying to pressure you into giving me special treatment. I just wish you'd act normal." Gilbert stood up and opened his arms. "So how about it?"

"Um... Okay."

He wasn't asking anything unusual of her. Just a normal hug. She got up from the sofa. Gilbert immediately wrapped Cecilia in his arms and slowly pulled her toward him in a gentle embrace that

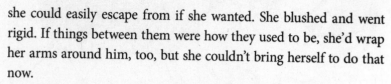

she could easily escape from if she wanted. She blushed and went rigid. If things between them were how they used to be, she'd wrap her arms around him, too, but she couldn't bring herself to do that now.

"So, Gil..."

"Yes?"

"It's true that I've been avoiding you on purpose because things have gotten complicated between us. And being close to you like this feels kind of...weird to me right now, you know?"

For some reason, admitting that made her feel like a loser. She heard Gilbert loudly exhale.

"You're anxious?"

"Um... Well... Yeah?"

She knew he had feelings for her; she couldn't let him hold her without feeling awkward about it.

"Well, I should be glad that you don't see me as just a friend, at least," said Gilbert, a hint of optimism in his voice.

Cecilia hung her head apologetically.

"I'm still not sure what you are to me. Sorry..."

His embrace grew a little tighter.

"No need to apologize. Take your time. I've been a brother to you for a long time, so I'm not expecting you to shift your perspective in just a few months. Besides, I'd be lying if I said I didn't enjoy the love you've been giving me as a sister, before you knew."

He finally released her.

"I won't pretend that I don't mind you choosing someone other than me, but I won't hold a grudge if you decide you only want me as a brother."

Cecilia understood that Gilbert didn't want her to choose him out of fear that it would be the only way to keep him in her life.

"Lean once told me that she despises how calculating I am."

"What?"

"Slyness and cunning are part of my nature, though. I'm unscrupulous in pursuing my desires."

"I think you're just very smart."

"'Manipulative' is the word you should be using." Gilbert laughed, amused by how Cecilia always tried to put a positive spin on everything. "But what I want is for you to be happy. And I'm perfectly willing to disregard other people's feelings, and my own, and even yours, if it's necessary to accomplish that."

"Wait, you'd disregard MY feelings, too?!"

"If I thought I needed to, sure. So think carefully about what you want. If you choose me in the end, I'll ensure you won't regret it."

"You're very confident…"

Gilbert's self-assured attitude kind of blew her away, and it hurt that she was so easy to read. She felt pathetic.

"You can hardly fault me for trying to impress the girl I love."

"You're so open about it!"

"There's no point in acting coy, is there?" he teased.

Cecilia cocked her head and pouted. Soon, however, her expression became apologetic once again.

"Gil…"

"Hmm?"

"I'm sorry for leaving you hanging."

"Don't be. You've given me more than you realize."

His warm and kind tone filled Cecilia with both guilt and gratitude at once. Not knowing what to say, she only nodded in response.

The shrine was haunted by the ghost of a nun.

* * *

Or at least, that was the rumor spreading lately among the nuns serving at the shrine. The specter was said to wander the hallways of the building at night without a lantern or any other source of light, so it was hard to spot. As for why it kept appearing, it was anyone's guess. Some witnesses had seen the spirit scraping at walls with her fingernails or standing in front of a door which had been sealed shut as long as anyone remembered—presumably because someone had died in the room it led to—muttering something.

"What if the ghost appears…?" asked a chestnut-haired nun in a trembling voice.

"Don't be daft," replied the nun she'd been paired with for their late-night patrol of the shrine. "That's just a made-up story."

"I can't stop being scared just because you tell me to! Doesn't that shadow over there look like a spirit watching us? And that one over there, like a person crouching?"

"S-stop it! Are you trying to make me afraid of shadows now?"

The two nuns started walking closer to each other.

The Church of Caritade preached that every soul went to the goddess' paradise after death, and that ghosts were mere superstition, but that wasn't stopping these nuns from being afraid of the supernatural.

"I want to get some shut-eye tonight, so stop talking about ghosts."

"But I can't stop thinking about them…"

Tap! A soft sound broke the silence of the sleeping shrine. As it continued, the nuns thought it was the sound of the other's footsteps on the marble floor at first. But then they noticed the rhythm didn't line up with their walking. They stopped in their tracks.

"Er, i-is someone else doing the rounds tonight besides us?"

"N-no, there shouldn't be..."

The two women didn't even notice that they'd joined hands. They both turned deathly pale, so frightened that their teeth were chattering. The sound was coming from where they were heading, and it was getting nearer and nearer.

Tap. Tap, tap. Tap, tap. The footsteps were unnervingly slow, but they were certainly getting louder... And then, a dark silhouette appeared at the edge of the ring of light shining from their lantern. The silhouette was unmistakable.

"It's... It's her..."

It was the silhouette of a nun, with the distinctive outline of the ankle-length tunic and the large bell-shaped wimple covering the head. The exact same habit the two patrolling nuns were wearing.

As the shape drew nearer, they glimpsed long golden locks. The mysterious woman wasn't carrying a lantern.

The two nuns clung to one another and screamed, shutting their eyes.

"Oh, good evening," came a polite greeting.

They opened their eyes again. This was no ghost.

"Lady Lean!"

It was the Holy Maiden candidate who the Holy Maiden herself had invited to the shrine. She was accompanied by a nun whose face they couldn't make out, as she had her head bent low. It was this nun they had mistaken for the ghost.

"Did we frighten you? I'm so sorry."

"N-no, we apologize for that unseemly reaction! But what might you be doing walking around the shrine so late at night?"

"I had the sudden need for a breath of fresh air," said Lean with a short laugh. She looked down at the ground. "The deep devotion of the sisters living at the shrine with the Holy Maiden, not to mention meeting the Holy Maiden herself, filled my heart with suffocating doubts as to whether I am a worthy candidate..."

"Oh..."

"I dared not go outside on my own at this hour, but this sister kindly offered to accompany me."

Lean gestured with her hand to the nun beside her, who bowed. She was still pointing her eyes humbly at the ground, but they could see her a little better now. Neither of the patrolling nuns recognized her, but there were so many women at the shrine they couldn't be familiar with everyone. For all they knew, she could have been a new recruit.

"Ah. Please do be careful on your walk."

"I will. I won't stay out long, so please don't worry about me."

Greatly relieved that they had encountered flesh-and-blood people instead of a specter, the two nuns smoothed out their habits and stood aside to let the pair pass.

"Thanks for the save, Lean!"

"Don't mention it. We were lucky they didn't alert anyone else."

"Yeah."

Lean and her blond companion—who was Cecilia, of course—also breathed a sigh of relief. They were, in fact, in the middle of a mission. The mission to obtain the Dirk of Destiny.

"How did you get your hands on the habit, though?"

"Oh, that was a piece of cake. I found out where the spares were stored and borrowed one for you on the way to meet up."

"I don't think it's called borrowing when you do it without permission..."

It had been clever of Lean to procure a disguise for Cecilia, but what if someone caught her rummaging through the nuns' wardrobe and making off with a habit? With her quick wits, Lean would have probably come up with a believable excuse, but it stressed Cecilia out to think of the risk.

On the other hand, Lean seemed completely nonchalant about the whole enterprise. As she was studying the instructions for getting to the underground room housing the Dirk of Destiny, she suddenly looked up at Cecilia.

"By the way, is Gil not taking part in the mission?"

"Oh, he is. He's covering for me, making sure nobody finds out I've left my room. We don't want the guys to come looking for me."

"Right, that's an important role, too."

The biggest threat in that regard was Jade. He was the most enthusiastic about getting the most out of the trip and had invited everyone to play board games in his room that night. Cecilia had politely declined, claiming she was too tired from walking around town all day, but knowing Jade, he might get the bright idea to come check in on her late at night. Cecilia delegated the duty of making him stay put to Gilbert, so he was now playing games with the others at Jade's.

"I was originally planning to have him act as a lookout in the hallway anyway."

"Oh?"

"To make sure nobody would see me skulking around dressed in a habit. I don't have to worry about Dante, but if Oscar and Jade saw me like this, it'd be game over."

Lean stroked her lower lip with her index finger, thinking.

"Hmm. Does it really matter if he finds out you're a girl now?"

"Huh?"

"You can't seriously be thinking that he'd kill you if he found out who you are. The Oscar from the game might, but 'our' Oscar is nothing like him."

"Um..."

Lean was right. Cecilia didn't fear Oscar would kill her...but that was no longer the problem. No, the issue was that she'd been friends with him as a guy for so long. She couldn't just go up to him and say, "By the way, I'm actually Cecilia! That doesn't change anything, right?"

He wouldn't kill me, but I bet he'd be so mad for having been duped...

Were he just an acquaintance, sure, she'd probably find it not too hard to tell him the truth. But they'd become rather good friends despite the fact she'd been using a fake identity the whole time. She imagined Oscar would feel betrayed if she revealed that their friendship was built on a lie.

"Well, if you want to still keep it a secret, that's fine by me. You don't have an obligation to tell him."

I don't have to tell him...

Lean's words absolved Cecilia of responsibility, but her conscience kept nagging at her.

"Right," she replied, eager to drop that topic.

About twenty minutes later, Lean and Cecilia made it into an inner section of the shrine. Most of the rooms in the vicinity seemed to be for storage, and there was nobody else around. Lean took the directions from Cecilia to check their location.

"Okay, so now... We've got to stomp three times on the third cobblestone from the wall at the end of this hallway, the one that's next to the vase..."

She went over to the cobblestone and stomped one, two, three times. The tile sank into the floor, and the wall in front of them started rumbling. It dipped a little at first, before moving to the side. They'd found a hidden door, and behind it was...

"A staircase!"

It led underground, presumably to where the Dirk of Destiny was kept.

The girls entered the secret stairway. There was a lantern on each side of the hidden door. When Lean lit them with her flintstone, the door slid back in place, concealing the entrance again. It seemed like magic, but perhaps there was just a clever trick to it.

They each took a lantern and began their descent down the spiral staircase. The sound of their footsteps on the stone echoed back at them.

"It's like a secret ninja house."

"More like an RPG dungeon, I'd say."

They didn't know why the original owner of the dagger felt the need to hide it from the world, but they sure had been determined.

Cecilia turned back to Lean to double-check the instructions.

"So next we light the candelabrum on the pedestal at the bottom of the stairs to open the final door?"

She got no response.

"Lean?"

"Huh? Oh, the candelabrum? Yes, that's right!"

"Is something wrong?"

Cecilia looked questioningly at her friend, who was staring at her lantern, lost in thought. Lean frowned and pointed to Cecilia's lamp.

"Do you notice anything strange?"

"About the lanterns?"

"Look at the top of the shade."

Cecilia examined her lamp but couldn't see anything unusual about it. What was Lean talking about?

"It looks like a normal lantern to me?"

"There's no dust on it."

"Er... So what?"

"If it's been sitting hidden behind a secret moving door for who knows how long, you'd expect it to be covered with a pile of dust, but it's clean. Almost like someone had used it recently."

"Holy smokes! You're right!"

A dreadful premonition overcame Cecilia for a moment, but she quickly dismissed it.

"Nah, no way. In the game, the protagonist is the first person to discover the dirk."

"That's what happens in the dating sim, yeah. If we are to trust how things play out there, we should be the only people here right now."

Cecilia felt cold sweat on her face. Could someone else have stumbled on this place, like the game's heroine? The possibility of that seemed slim, but it wasn't zero. That being said, the discovery of the Dirk of Destiny would have been huge, and yet nobody had heard anything about it, Lean and Cecilia included.

"Let's hurry up and find the dagger."

"Yeah."

They started running down the stairs. Soon, they could see the pedestal with the candelabrum at the bottom...

"It's already lit!"

"Cecilia, over here!" Lean, the first to get to the bottom of the stairs, called her over.

She was standing in front of a wide-open stone door.

"It's gone..."

Cecilia followed Lean's gaze into the room past the entrance. Inside was a statue of the goddess with a pedestal in front of it. There was a dagger-shaped indentation on the pedestal, but the dirk itself was conspicuously absent.

"Who took it...?"

Cecilia stepped toward the door, as if in a daze, and felt something under her shoe. Moving her foot back, she noticed something sparkly on the floor. She crouched down to pick it up.

"Lean, I found an earring."

It looked familiar, but Cecilia couldn't figure out where she'd seen it before. Her friend, on the other hand, recognized it immediately.

"I think that's Prince Janis'!"

"What?!"

"Prince Janis stole the dirk…"

They looked at each other.

A little while before Cecilia and Lean found Prince Janis' earring in the underground chamber, the boys met up in Jade's room to play board games. There were five of them: Jade, Gilbert, Oscar, Huey, and Dante. Neither Gilbert nor Huey really wanted to be there, though. Only Jade and Dante were excited for game night, while Oscar joined them purely because he had nothing better to do.

They were sitting around a circular table. Jade had a tower of board games from different countries next to him on the floor. Board games had been his special interest before he got into BL romance, and he'd amassed quite an impressive collection, finding rare gems as he traveled to different lands on business.

"A country's culture and customs are reflected in its board games, so you can learn a lot from them. And talking about business goes more smoothly over a game," Jade explained when his friends arrived.

Once they sat down, he was in no hurry to open any of them, though.

"Now that I've got you all here, I'd love to talk about stuff we don't normally get to!"

"I thought you invited us over to play games together?"

"We'll do that, too! But the real treat tonight will be having some deep conversations!"

"What do we normally not have a chance to talk about?" Oscar raised an eyebrow.

"It's not like we don't often get together like this. I mean, we're all living in a dorm, right?" Huey poured cold water over the fired-up Jade.

"My thoughts exactly," added Gilbert.

"You guys! Don't be such party poopers!"

"What do you want to talk about, specifically? Is there something you wanted to discuss with us?"

"I hadn't thought about that but, actually, how about this! Do you guys have anyone you like? You know, in *that* way?"

Oscar had a sudden coughing fit.

"That's your idea of a 'deep conversation?'" Huey groaned with visible distaste.

Jade furrowed his brow, reconsidering.

"Hmm. You know what, forget that one! Let's drop it."

"Oh? Why?" Dante looked at him quizzically.

Jade touched his forehead as if he had a headache.

"If I had you talk about your love interests out loud, that would make your choices official, and it could hurt the feelings of less mainstream pairing enthusiasts. It's sometimes better not to make things official to keep the imagination unfettered…"

"Gilbert, do you understand a word of what he's saying?" asked Oscar.

"No, and I'm glad for it."

"Lean's influence has corrupted him," Dante said with a chuckle.

Jade was of course referring to Oscar and Gilbert making it clear who they had the hots for. He'd used to be an ardent supporter of the Gilbert x Cecil pairing, but lately he'd been leaning toward Gilbert x Oscar. As long as neither of the guys brought up their preferences, he was free to dream and let his mind explore any gutter it fancied.

Wind taken out of his sails, Jade slumped over the table.

"I was planning for this to be a get-to-know-each-other-better night, but it's not going so well."

"Maybe instead of trying to force a topic, we could just get started playing games? And chat about things that come up spontaneously?"

"Besides, we already know each other pretty well, don't we?"

"You think so, Oscar?"

Jade seemed not unpleasantly surprised.

"I have an idea that I think you guys will love!" Dante piped up.

His cheerfulness made Huey wary.

"Somehow I doubt it…," he murmured.

Dante ignored him and carried on in a louder voice.

"It's a subject we can't discuss with ladies around, so it's perfect for male bonding!"

"What is it, what is it?" Jade leaned toward Dante, dying of curiosity.

Dante smiled wider.

"Let's talk about which parts of women's bodies we like best!"

"Er…"

"Like, are you a boob person or a butt person?"

"Enough, Dante!" Gilbert's voice was like a whip. He scrunched up his face and glared at Dante with contempt. "Is this all you can think about?"

"What's wrong with it? Isn't it a fun topic for us guys?"

"You need to stop objectifying people, Dante." Oscar wouldn't have any of it either.

Dante pouted, but for better or for worse, it wasn't in his nature to go down without a fight.

"Okay, forget body parts, then. How about situations? Like when a girl looks up at you, or ties her hair in a ponytail?"

"Oh, I see what you mean!" Jade perked up, happy to finally be able to rejoin the conversation. "I think it's really cute when girls undo their braids."

"That's a good one! Personally, I prefer the reverse. There's something sexy about women braiding their hair!"

"I guess so! I also think it's so cute when they rub their eyes sleepily."

"Oh, yeah! Especially when you're the only other person to know the reason why they didn't get enough sleep, heh-heh."

Despite their very different personalities, Dante and Jade were really hitting it off. Dante turned to his underling, Huey, who was watching them with a look of irritation on his face.

"Your turn, Huey."

"For what?"

"To talk about situations that tickle your fancy! We're not letting you off the hook this time!"

Huey grimaced, not wanting to participate, but Dante kept staring at him expectantly.

"I like when girls...smile."

Dante was quiet for a moment...

"Bwa-ha-ha-ha! It doesn't take much for you, huh? You crack me up!"

Huey's cheeks reddened slightly.

"That's too basic to count as a situation, don't you think? But I see why you said that. All it takes to warm your heart is for Lean to give you a little grin—am I right? You're head over heels for her. How cute."

"You've become such a moron since joining the academy," Huey growled, shaking with anger.

"Sorry if I hurt your feelings," Dante replied without a shred of guilt in his voice. Then he turned his attention to Oscar and Gilbert. "And you two? Let me guess, Gilbert. I bet that unlike Huey, you like to see girls in tears."

"Excuse me?!" Gilbert raised his voice, offended by the unjust suggestion.

Huey, far from sympathizing with Gilbert and showing him support as a fellow victim of Dante's mockery, raised his hand like a pupil in class.

"As in, teasing a girl he likes until she's in tears?"

"No, Gilbert wouldn't be teasing her. He'd be talking her down." Jade joined in on the assault.

Encouraged by having two people side with him, Dante went for the kill.

"You'd crush her with your rhetoric, and once she broke out in tears, you'd gently wipe them off her pretty face. You calculating bastard!"

"Yeah, that's mean."

"But if she left him for good after he made her cry so much, he'd be furious! Even though it'd be his own fault for testing the limits of her love... For manipulating her feelings... For letting her love ferment into hatred, the dam of loyalty bursting as her heart overflows with hurt... Hold on! I'm onto something here! This could be a masterpiece!" Jade got himself worked up as his imagination ran wild.

Gilbert lost his patience.

"I can't believe how nasty you all are, projecting onto me like that! I don't derive joy from making girls cry, just so you know!" He turned to Oscar for support, who'd been sitting in silence.

"You've known me longer than they do, Your Highness. You can vouch for my good character!"

"That...explains so much. Poor Cecilia..."

"What? Not you, too..."

Gilbert felt utterly betrayed. Oscar was staring at him in disbelief, covering his mouth with his hand.

The reason he was often harsh toward Cecilia wasn't that he liked to see her in tears—it was because he had to be strict with her to stop her from doing dumb things that would land her in trouble. He did find it cute when she was crying, but that was unrelated. Or... was it?

To his relief, however, Gilbert didn't have much time for introspection, as Dante spotted some new prey.

"And what about you, Oscar?"

"Hmm..." The prince crossed his arms, thinking. "Nothing comes to mind, really..."

"Perhaps you need a more concrete example. What would you find cute if Cecilia did it?"

Oscar looked up when he heard his fiancée's name, finally interested in the conversation.

Jade turned to Huey.

"He means Gil's older sister, right? The girl we met when we visited?"

"I'd think so."

"Ah, right. I totally forgot she's Oscar's fiancée! I don't know much about her, but she's very pretty, isn't she?"

"Did she crush your fantasies?" Huey asked, knowing that Jade shipped Oscar with Gilbert.

Jade shook his head.

"Not at all! You've got to keep an open mind, you know? A fiancée doesn't mean it's a done deal!"

"So…being broad-minded means not putting much stock in engagements?"

"It's something I learned from Lean! If you're going for a non-canon pairing, you can't be a stickler for details!"

"What a mentor, that Lean…," Huey said with sarcasm.

Meanwhile, Oscar was still stuck for an answer. Dante stared at him, urging him to come up with something.

"Has she never given you a jolt of excitement?"

"Well…"

"Maybe it was something she said? Or something she did?"

Oscar blushed, like Dante's leading questions had stirred a very personal memory. Gilbert caught onto this, and it pissed him off. He didn't want Oscar thinking those sorts of things about "his" Cecilia.

The prince spent a few more minutes in deep thought, blushing all the while, before finally speaking.

"I suppose I do enjoy holding hands."

"Holding hands?"

"Basic."

Oscar's prolonged pondering had led Jade and Huey to expect something quirky or even raunchy, so they were severely disappointed. Dante wagged his pointer finger at them.

"No, no, you shouldn't take it literally! I've known Oscar for a long time, and the workings of his mind are no mystery to me! Allow me to elucidate this for you!"

"Okay?"

"What Oscar likes is…when ladies initiate physical contact!"

"Ah, so he wants to be groped?"

"Oh, is that his kink?"

Jade's curious look and Huey's mocking stare gave Oscar a head rush.

"No, that's not what I said!"

"We were talking about innocent little situations and mannerisms we like, and here you share with us that you're into being groped. You closet perv, you!"

"You're overstepping your bounds, Dante. Stop making fun of me!"

"Your Highness, please see me in my room after this. We need to talk," Gilbert said with a dark smile.

"Gilbert, I honestly wasn't talking or thinking about groping! You have to believe me!"

"You can elaborate on your excuses when we have our discussion later. Besides, you've already lost my trust today."

"I'm not making excuses!"

Gilbert was fuming as Oscar fumbled over his words in an attempt to defend himself, while Dante kept adding fuel to the fire. Jade and Huey joined the banter every now and again. They were all having fun, for the most part, and time passed far too quickly.

Two days after failing to retrieve the Dirk of Destiny from the shrine, Cecilia paid a visit to Grace in Vleugel Academy's research facility.

"You're saying there's a high chance that the Dirk of Destiny has fallen into Prince Janis' clutches?"

"I'm afraid so."

Grace stroked her chin, a grim look on her face, while Cecilia sat in front of her with her head hung low. Then Cecilia thought of something and leaned forward toward Grace.

"Did something like this happen in any of the game scenarios?"

"No. In most of them, the existence of the dirk is unconfirmed. Nobody even knows what it looks like until the heroine finds it, and Doctor Mordred is the first to discover what it does and how to wield it."

Which meant that only transmigrated players of *Vleugel Academy 3* might have known where to go looking for the dagger...

"Wait, so does that mean Janis is also a transmigration of someone from our old world?"

"We can't rule that out, but there *is* another possibility."

"What's that?"

"There were signs of a burglary in Mordred's office on Advent Day. One of his research papers was stolen."

"Holy...!"

This was the first Cecilia was hearing of this. Grace told her that even Mordred didn't immediately notice that anything had gone missing. He was working on a thesis titled "The Underlying Cause of the Obstructions," and the Dirk of Destiny was mentioned in his research notes.

"The documents were later found in the office next door, so suspicion naturally fell on the researcher who had been using it, but they might have been working for Janis."

The suspect had been captured but denied the accusation.

"Do you think Janis instigated the Advent Day riot to distract us while one of his pawns stole the research papers?"

"Maybe, but I'm leaning toward it being a secondary objective after eliminating the Holy Maiden candidate."

Grace picked up the earring from her desk and held it up in the light.

"There's no shortage of researchers investigating the Obstructions in our country. It would be in Prince Janis' best interest to keep tabs on their findings, since he has the power to manipulate Obstructions according to his will. For all we know, the existence of the Dirk of Destiny might have surprised him, too."

An item which could remove permanently remove the Obstructions from this world was a grave threat to Janis. Naturally, he would want to find it at all costs to prevent anyone from using it.

Cecilia agreed with Grace's reasoning for the most part, but something still didn't add up.

"But hold on, Mordred only wrote about how the Dirk of Destiny was supposed to be used. He never had the information on where to find it."

"This can be explained in one of two ways. The less likely explanation is that Prince Janis is a transmigration of someone from our world, as you suggested earlier. But I reckon that he might have chanced upon ancient records describing the dirk and where it was hidden."

Grace swept her eyes from the earring to Cecilia.

"If you still want to exorcise the Obstructions from this world, you have but one option."

"Just one…?"

"You will have to retrieve the Dirk of Destiny from Prince Janis, and you must do this in time for the Selection Ceremony on the last day of March—your next, and last, chance to visit the shrine."

→ ⑨ ←

"That's easier said than done…"

Three days later, Cecilia was sitting on a bench in the academy courtyard after classes, ruminating over what to do. It was a sunny autumnal day, but the breeze was chilly. That should have come as no surprise, though, since it was almost the end of November.

Cecilia looked up from the ground and sighed.

"I've got to find Prince Janis somehow, but how do I even do that?"

Grace had told her to find him, but didn't give her any instructions or hints, and Cecilia didn't have a clue how to reach him. She'd only spoken to him once, and she hadn't known who he was at the time.

What aliases was he going by? Where was he staying? Had he gone back to his home country already?

Gil said he's looking into it, but he hasn't made any progress so far. Is there nothing I can do by myself?

Gilbert had explicitly instructed her to leave this matter to him, believing it was too dangerous for Cecilia to get involved in. She understood that Prince Janis was not to be trifled with, and was grateful that her brother cared so much for her, but sitting around twiddling her thumbs was one of the hardest things in the world for her.

Maybe I could look for clues in some way Gilbert wouldn't disapprove of?

"What are you up to, Cecil?"

Cecilia was so lost in thought she hadn't noticed she was no longer alone. Two students, traces of childlike innocence still on their faces, their hair braided in opposite directions, had come into the garden.

"Eins and Zwei!"

"It's been a while."

"Good to see you again."

Eins gave her a little wave while Zwei smiled bashfully. Cecilia got up from the bench and ran over to them.

"Wow, it feels like it's been ages since I last saw you two! Was everything okay back home?" Cecilia asked uneasily.

The twins had been summoned back home after Advent Day. Their father, Duke Machias, was one of the special guests Lean had invited to see the play at the orphanage, but he'd chosen the worst time possible to show up: when Zwei temporarily lost his sanity, and the show had to be called off. The duke, who had made the trip without telling anyone and was eager to see his sons on stage without causing them undue anxiety, must have been rather bemused by that state of affairs.

"Before we went home, we had no idea that Father was there when you went missing and everyone was frantically searching for you… He had a lot of questions for us, and he didn't ask them nicely. He even struck Zwei…"

"What?! He hit you, Zwei?!"

"It wasn't that bad…"

Zwei instinctively rubbed his left cheek, remembering the pain. It wasn't bruised but looked a bit red. On closer observation, the left corner of his lips also seemed tender. Had it gotten split from a punch to the face?

"Dad just hit him once, and afterward he even muttered an apology for not having done anything to help Zwei with his anxieties. He's not heartless, you know. And he understood that he only acted that way because he was possessed by an Obstruction," Eins said resolutely.

"If you say so…"

"The letter you sent also helped to quell his anger. Thanks for that."

"Yes, thank you so much, Cecil!"

"Oh, don't mention it!" She waved her hand.

She'd already been writing a letter to Duke Machias when she heard that the twins had been called home immediately. In the message, Cecilia reassured the duke that she was unharmed and asked him not to punish Zwei in light of the difficult circumstances. She hadn't known whether it would make a difference, but sending it was better than doing nothing.

"Dad said he wanted to pay a visit to your family to offer a formal apology."

"Wait, what?"

"So let us know what day would suit you."

Cecilia tensed up. This would be a problem. House Admina didn't actually exist, so there was nowhere for the Duke to visit.

Cecilia broke out in cold sweat. She shook her head.

"Please tell your dad there's no need for that."

"But…"

"My home isn't really suitable for hosting someone as grand as a duke. I'd only feel embarrassed. Please just tell him not to worry about it."

"All right, it's fine if you'd prefer he not come."

Cecilia went weak with relief when Eins said that. She didn't care about Duke Machias apologizing anyway. She was just glad that the twins were back. When they'd departed, Zwei said he wasn't sure he would be allowed to return to the academy, so they might not see each other again. That had made her worried sick. Befriending them was no easy task, and she would have been heartbroken to lose them so soon.

"And what about you? Did you get in trouble?" asked Eins.

"What, me?"

Eins raised an eyebrow at her and crossed his arms.

"Yeah? Have they been badgering you since?"

"Who?"

"Gil and Oscar, who else?"

She noted that Eins shortened Gilbert's name. The twins were no longer outsiders—they were a part of her inner circle now.

"Ah! No, it's all good! They told me off for being so reckless, but that's a closed chapter now!"

"That's it? They just told you off?"

"Yeah. They kept me for like an hour after that dinner, lecturing me on my irresponsible behavior. I get that they were worried sick about me, so I'll have to be more careful in the future."

If she were to travel back in time, she would make the same choices all over again. Cecilia did feel sorry about worrying her friends, but she had no regrets.

"Even after all that happened, you're still talking to us."

"Of course I am. You're fun to be around!" she said with a big smile.

The twins, who had seemed a little anxious before, finally relaxed.

"So, anyway, did you come here to hang out?" Cecilia changed the topic.

Eins and Zwei exchanged glances and nodded at each other before turning back toward her.

"We came here looking for you, actually."

"Oh?"

"We wanted to tell you about something we discovered."

Their tone grew serious.

"While we were back home, we asked Dad and our servants about the man who stayed at Cuddy's house five years ago, before our mother was murdered. The man who resembled Prince Janis."

Cecilia opened her eyes wide and held her breath for a few seconds.

"His name was Jil Versul, eighteen years old. One of the servants heard him talking to someone about being on the way to Algram."

If he was eighteen then, then he'd be twenty-three now, which matched Prince Janis' current age.

Zwei picked up where Eins left off.

"This Jil arrived at Cuddy's house two days before Mother was murdered, and left on the day of the crime. It's been five years since it happened, but everyone still remembers it like it was yesterday."

Zwei frowned as he said that, perhaps having flashbacks to that time himself. Unlike the last time they'd talked about his mother's murder, he didn't seem so vulnerable. He had finally processed the horrors of that day and could now talk about it without losing composure. Perhaps surviving the crisis on Advent Day led him to finding new resilience and determination.

"We asked Dad to see if he could find any other information about Jil Versul, and he managed to hit on something. About three months ago, someone bribed the guards at a northern checkpoint on the border with Nortracha, and two men were smuggled into the country."

"And Jil Versul was one of them?"

"Correct. And his description matches up with Prince Janis, who we met in Algram."

The hair on the back of Cecilia's neck stood up. There she had it—Janis was using the alias Jil Versul. That should be enough information to track down where he was staying, but she'd have to act fast.

Once I find his current location, I'll have to catch him before he moves on...

He probably wouldn't be staying at one place for very long, and for all she knew, he might be staying at a different lodging every night. It would be a huge waste of time and effort to track down which inn he was staying at, only to discover he'd already left.

As it turned out, Eins and Zwei had already taken initiative in this matter.

"We have the name of the lodging he's been using and may still be staying at."

"Really?!"

"He sent a letter to the checkpoint guards he bribed thanking them for their 'kindness' and letting them know he'll need another favor soon."

"We finally managed to trace back to where the letter was sent from this morning. It's an inn in Algram."

Zwei showed Cecilia the message. She took the envelope from him, noticing that it contained a small object in addition to the note itself. She shook it out onto her hand.

"He enclosed a ring with the letter?"

"Yes. It's made from malachite."

Cecilia held up the green ring to the sunshine. It was pretty, but didn't seem to be worth much, so it couldn't serve as a form of payment to the crooked guards.

"We wanted to tell you that we're going to that inn now."

"Wait, are you serious?!"

"Totally. We want to question him about what happened to Cuddy. It doesn't make sense for him to have done what he did. He was a devout believer, but he wasn't a killer."

"We're pretty sure Janis made him do it somehow."

Beads of cold sweat rolled down Cecilia's cheeks. The twins didn't know yet that Janis could make Obstructions possess people. If they went to meet him on their own, Janis could set another Obstruction on Zwei, and his brother, too.

"We're aware of the scary rumors about him, so we'll pick a busy spot with lots of potential witnesses and be very careful around him. But just in case we don't come back—"

"No, don't do it!" Cecilia screamed, cutting Zwei off.

The brothers looked at her in surprise.

"I understand that this is very important to you, but you can't just go like this, without a plan, and a backup plan, and—"

"We can't afford to wait. Otherwise, he may be gone by the time we get there."

"He wrote in the letter that he'd be needing a favor from the checkpoint guards soon. He's preparing to leave the country."

Those were solid arguments, and Cecilia didn't know what else to say. They were absolutely right, and she'd been thinking pretty much the same just a minute ago. This might be the twins' only shot at confronting Janis directly.

She wanted to go with them. Partly out of concern for their safety, but also to fulfill her own objective—snagging the Dirk of Destiny off him. This was her chance, too.

There's a problem, though...

She couldn't go now because Gilbert wasn't around. He'd told her when they were having lunch that he'd be going somewhere after classes to investigate something in relation to Janis. She wasn't expecting him to be back anytime soon. He might have only left recently, in fact. He'd also said:

"You stay put until I come back, okay?"

She'd promised to wait patiently for his return. Going with Eins and Zwei to meet Janis at some inn was the exact opposite.

This is the worst possible timing...

She looked up at the two brothers, their faces and expressions identical.

Those two are going, no matter what.

She could see unshakable resolve in their eyes. They'd been thinking about this for a long time, days even, and had made up their minds about confronting Janis. She could ask them to wait all she wanted, but they weren't going to listen.

They were ignorant of the scale of danger Janis posed to them. Even if Cecilia told them now that Janis could summon Obstructions at will and make them possess people, they might not believe her. And if they did, it might make them even more insistent on pressing him for answers.

Cecilia took a deep breath in and slowly exhaled. Sometimes you had to take your chances, despite the risks.

"All right. But I'm going with you."

"What?" they asked simultaneously, taken completely by surprise.

"Why would you—"

"There's something I need to ask Prince Janis, too! So please, take me along!"

"But what if something happened to you...?"

"Look, I understand what I'm signing up for." Cecilia clenched her hands into fists. "I just need to do something real quick to prep, okay?"

They left the academy grounds an hour later. The city was as busy as ever, with pedestrians milling around and countless stores beckoning them in. The cobblestone main roads were lined with cafés and stores with souvenirs for tourists, while the central square was a hub for stallkeepers loudly advertising their wares.

Cecilia, Eins, and Zwei took the back alleys to arrive an area with a very different atmosphere. There were homeless people curled up with their backs against the walls, and the women waiting outside lodgings didn't look like customers. The squalid look of the place was compounded by a stench rising from the gutters. It didn't feel safe to be walking there.

"You sure you've got the right address?" Cecilia asked, voice wavering.

She was clinging to Eins's arm. Zwei, who answered her, was clinging to his other arm.

"Yes, it's around here. It doesn't look like somewhere a prince would be staying, does it…"

"No kidding…"

"Can't you two just walk normally? Let go of me, you're going to stretch out my sleeves."

Only Eins was unfazed. Even though he looked exactly like Zwei, their personalities couldn't be more different.

He kept checking the signboards of the cheap inns and hostels they were passing by.

"It's got to be close…"

"What's your plan for when we find the inn, Eins? Do we hide and wait outside until he comes out?"

"What? No, we go right in."

"Huh?!"

"We might be waiting forever if we do that!"

Zwei smiled awkwardly at Cecilia.

"I also suggested to him that we should try to ambush Janis."

They kept on walking through the maze of seedy alleyways, but now the twins had taken up the front, with Cecilia bringing up the rear. They were getting used to the grimy look of this part of the city, so their steps had gotten lighter, more assured. Eins, who hadn't been tense to begin with, even got chatty.

"You know, I'm not even that worried about Janis. His bodyguard, though..."

"I remember his menacing stare. I guess we'll have to get rid of him somehow, or he won't let us talk to the prince."

Ah, right!

Cecilia looked up from the ground, thinking that she should probably tell the twins about Janis' ability to manipulate Obstructions. Even if they didn't quite believe her now, it might still make them more cautious.

"Hey—," she called out to them, but before she got the chance finish her sentence, someone grabbed her by the arm and pulled her off to the side, into an alley so dark she couldn't see where it ended. The attacker placed a hand over her mouth while holding her from behind with the other arm. Her legs were free, so she geared up to step on the kidnapper's foot, putting her full weight behind it...

"I'd appreciate it if you didn't do that," came a soft, yet dignified voice.

She craned her neck to get a look at the man behind her. He let go of her and put his hands up in the air, as if surrendering.

"Unlike the local princes, I'm not a strong fighter."

He took a few steps back and smiled at Cecilia. She gasped.

"Prince Janis…"

"Oh, please call me Janis. Or Jil, if you prefer."

He knew. Had this whole thing with the letter been a setup to lure them here? Had they waltzed into his trap?

What have…we done…?

He'd played them like pawns.

Janis half-turned away from the horrified Cecilia.

"I'm sorry for having been so indelicate. All I wanted was to invite you for tea, just the two of us. You'll come with me, won't you, Cecil?"

She didn't respond.

"Come with me of your own free will and I'll leave those two alone."

She followed his gaze. Eins and Zwei had noticed she wasn't walking behind them anymore and were looking around for her, alarmed.

"Please take a seat. Would you like coffee? Or tea?"

She just glared at Janis.

"Oh, don't worry. The café staff don't work for me. They won't poison your drink."

He had led her to one of the cafés on the main street. They were sitting at a table outside, Cecilia sending him a glare of hostility, him smiling back.

Janis raised his hand to get the staff's attention and ordered two teas.

"Try to relax a little, will you? I won't eat you. What I'd like is to have a chat with you."

"About what?"

"Well, didn't you have something you wanted to talk to me about yourself?"

She looked at him with undisguised suspicion. Janis smiled even wider, as if he either didn't notice her expression or simply didn't care.

"It was only the Machias brothers I indirectly invited, but you turned up as well. You must have been very eager to see me."

"What did you invite them for?"

"First, you tell me what it is you want from me."

Cecilia glared at him with even more angry defiance when he deflected her question. Then Janis treated her to another big grin, as if to mock her. He leaned in close, stopping his face inches from hers, and brushed a strand of hair from the side of his cheek to tuck it behind his ear. A drop-shaped earring was dangling from it.

"I'm guessing you might have found an earring just like this one?"

Cecilia stared wordlessly.

"Ha-ha, I knew it!"

He'd noticed how she tensed up at the question, confirming his suspicions.

"Did you leave it there on purpose? So I would come looking for you?" Cecilia asked in a low voice.

"No, no, I never intended for you to find it. The person I was hoping to lure was the Holy Maiden candidate—what's her name, Lean? Not that I care too much that she didn't come, since that was just a minor side project of mine. It's you knights that I'm more interested in now."

"What?"

"I was going to make a special request of the Machias twins today, but since you're here, it might be more fun to ask you instead." Janis put one knee over the other, crossed his arms, leaned on the

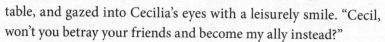

table, and gazed into Cecilia's eyes with a leisurely smile. "Cecil, won't you betray your friends and become my ally instead?"

"Huh?"

"Join me, Cecil."

His proposition was so preposterous she could only stare at him, gaping. The emotion behind Janis' smile was unreadable to her. He tilted his neck, looking at her expectantly. Cecilia had no idea how to respond. She pinched the bridge of her nose, thinking.

"I don't understand what you want from me. I'm not going to betray my friends."

"Now, now, don't shoot me down without hearing the details. That's not good negotiation. I'm not asking you to stab your dear friends in the back or anything so drastic, but I would appreciate you sharing some information with me."

"I'm not going to—"

"I won't tell anyone that you're a traitor. Pinky swear."

"The answer is NO!"

"I'd be so grateful for your help that I'd even give you a present afterward. How about the Dirk of Destiny?"

Just as Cecilia had been ready to reiterate her firm refusal, the words got caught in her throat. Realizing she'd stood up from her chair in agitation, she sat back down.

"It would be my reward to you, contingent on my plans succeeding. How about it? Not a bad deal, right? I know you've been searching for it, too, since you found my missing earring."

"..."

"Well? What do you say to that?"

Cecilia took a deep breath and sighed. She hesitated for a moment before speaking.

"What are these plans of yours?"

"Exacting revenge against the Church of Caritade."

"What did they do to you?"

"It's not what they did to me—it's what they did to everyone. They're responsible for infecting the world with Obstructions."

Cecilia gasped. Watching her out of the corner of his eye, Janis continued.

"To be more precise, it's the system that's to blame, not any individuals. In fact, there may no longer be anyone who understands how it works. Yet it is undeniable that the Church of Caritade is behind establishing the system which conjures the Obstructions, and I want to put an end to it."

"What are you talking about?"

"The Obstructions are part of the system designed to identify the Holy Maiden candidates."

Cecilia tilted her head, confused. Janis raised his index finger and explained things to her, as if he were lecturing a child.

"You've been raised to think of Obstructions as parasitic entities or ghosts that possess people, but that's not what they are at all. They're more like seeds, and everyone in the Prosper Kingdom has one dormant inside them. They've been planted in you without your knowledge."

"And these seeds sprout into Obstructions?"

"Not always."

"What else can happen?"

"I told you, their role is to reveal the Holy Maiden candidates."

Cecilia opened her eyes wide in shock as the truth dawned on her.

"The Obstructions are a side effect. The seeds bloom in Holy Maiden candidates, manifesting as flower-shaped marks on their bodies. But sometimes, they germinate in people who are not suitable candidates, and then they grow into ugly vines—Obstructions."

So the Church of Caritade was somehow planting these seeds in people to discern who was suitable to become the next Holy Maiden, and sometimes those who didn't qualify had Obstructions grow in them as a side effect? How would they do that, though?

If what he's saying is true, this changes everything...

Everyone believed that the Obstructions emerged near the time of the Selection Ceremony due to the weakening of the Holy Maiden's powers, but if Janis was right, it was actually because the time had come for the seeds to germinate.

"The Selection Ceremony should be called the Pruning, really. What you're doing is removing the superfluous flowers until only the most beautiful remains. That way it will have all the nutrients to itself, thriving better than if it had to share the resources." Janis laughed, finding it funny that the Church of Caritade was applying the principles of horticulture to human beings. "The seeds won't germinate in most people, and they'll live out their lives none the wiser. Don't you find this practice cruel? The Church exposes innocent people to danger to ensure the survival of their faith."

Sacrificing people just to keep their institution going—of course it sounded wicked and inhumane. But Cecilia wasn't yet convinced whether Janis' tale was true or just something he'd made up. It did sound plausible, and it would explain a lot, but she only had the prince's word to go on. There was no proof.

"Why are you telling me all this?" she asked cautiously.

Janis flashed her a disarming smile.

"Because I'd like you on my side. You have a strong sense of right and wrong. I thought that if you knew the truth, you might naturally want to cooperate with me."

"Why should I believe you?"

"You'll have to decide for yourself whether you believe me or not."

Janis appeared to consider something for a moment before leaning closer and telling her something in a conspiratorial whisper:

"I'll let you in on a secret. I have the ability to make the seeds of Obstructions bloom."

She was surprised that he'd voluntarily disclosed this information, but it wasn't shocking to her in the slightest. Cecilia neither gasped nor expressed disbelief upon hearing the truth. This puzzled Janis.

"Hold on... This isn't news to you, is it? You knew?"

"Um..."

"Well, I'll be damned. You're more observant than I took you for. I suppose you figured it out on Advent Day."

She hadn't really figured it out by herself, but she wasn't going to correct him.

"And do you know why I have that ability?"

"How would I?"

"Let me tell you, then. It's because I'm a descendant of Lumiel, the first Holy Maiden."

Now this was a bolt from the blue for Cecilia. She gasped and froze for a second, forgetting to even breathe. Her reaction didn't escape the prince's notice.

"This part of history might have been erased in your country, but Nortracha was founded by Lumiel's son, who was expelled from the Kingdom of Prosper." Janis gestured with his hand for emphasis. "He was originally supposed to take over the Holy Maiden's duties, but was born without any powers. His body lacked a special mark. Persecuted, he was forced to leave the country, but he wanted to remain close to his homeland. Hence, he established a nation of his own next to Prosper. Now you know why I'm rather knowledgeable about the Obstructions, and the Holy Maidens. And why I can even make Obstructions grow within people. Quite the party trick for the prince of Nortracha, don't you think?" he chuckled.

He uncrossed his legs and crossed them the other way, then reclined in his chair so that he was no longer in Cecilia's face.

"Now that I've explained everything, do you trust me at least a little bit more?"

Cecilia sat in silence, staring at him.

"Good."

Janis gave her an easy smile and extended his hand, as if he wanted her to shake it.

"Nortracha and Prosper are sister nations. I hate to see your citizens needlessly suffering at the hands of the Church of Caritade. Help me end this, Cecil."

She said nothing.

"You who are taking part in the Selection Ceremony have the most up-to-date information about the Church. I'm not interested in learning of your private affairs. What I'm hoping to get from you is leads which will help me destroy the Church."

She still wasn't talking and instead stared at the table.

"Cecil?" Janis tried to get her attention.

She didn't seem to hear him at first, but after another prolonged moment of silence, she looked up and met his gaze.

"You're lying."

"Oh?"

"I don't know if what you said about the Church is true or not. Maybe it is. But you're lying about your objective."

"What makes you think so?"

"The fact that you stole the Dirk of Destiny for yourself. You would have given it to us if you both knew its purpose and wanted the Church out of the picture," Cecilia said quietly.

Janis withdrew his extended hand.

"I didn't know you were searching for the dirk as well. I went ahead and stole it from the shrine to give it to you later. I should've made that clear, I suppose. I did promise to give it to you—"

"As a reward for helping you realize your goal. Which doesn't make sense. Neither do any of your other actions until now that I'm aware of."

"I'll explain everything later. I had good reasons for getting in your way earlier. I'm sure you'll find them understandable..."

"How are you going to explain away trying to get Oscar assassinated?"

Janis finally fell silent. For just a moment, all emotion drained from his face, leaving behind the calculating coldness of a self-serving politician, but he quickly covered it up with a friendly smile.

"Ah, so you knew about that," he muttered with disappointment.

Cecilia wasn't finished.

"It's not the Church of Caritade you hate, is it? It's this country."

Her words sent him into a paroxysm of quiet, but uncontrollable giggling. When at last he spoke, he was struggling to suppress giggles.

"Score! I like smart people. You're absolutely right! I despise the Prosper Kingdom, and I'm going to wipe it off the map. I'll destroy its royal family, I'll kill all its citizens, and I'll even erase its religion."

"..."

"Man, I thought my improvised story was pretty good. You seemed so simple-minded, so I was sure you'd buy it on the spot, but I guess I should've put in some effort into coming up with a better lie. You leave me no choice but to go with my original strategy." He opened his arms with palms raised. "Will you please become my ally, Cecil? Or will I have to germinate the seeds of Obstructions in everyone around us to convince you?"

Cecilia grimaced, revolted by the nonchalance with which he threatened her.

"You were going to intimidate Eins and Zwei like this, too?"

"Not necessarily. They're so close, aren't they? The younger brother is codependent, while the older is fiercely protective. I would only need to take one hostage to easily manipulate the other."

"Was Cuddy Miland among the people whose Obstructions you germinated?"

"Sorry, who?"

"The servant who killed Eins and Zwei's mother."

"Hmm…" Janis stroked his chin. "I can't say I remember him. It was so long ago, you know. I make a rule of quickly forgetting names of people who are irrelevant to my life, because what's the point in remembering?"

"I see."

"Anyway, will you answer me now? Are we going to become friends or not? I can make those seeds sprout with a touch of my finger." He wiggled his digits. "Or would you like to experience what it's like to become host to an Obstruction yourself?"

Janis reached out toward Cecilia, but before he could touch her, someone slapped his hand away.

"Huh?!"

"Keep your dirty paws off my princess."

Dante had materialized out of thin air behind Cecilia. He wrapped an arm around her protectively and stared at Janis with a mocking smile playing on his lips.

"Long time no see, Prince Janis."

"Why, if it isn't Dante Hampton. Good to see you, traitor."

"I see you didn't come looking for me without taking precautions."

Janis appeared rather pleased as he rubbed the hand Dante had struck.

"Why is this a surprise to you?" Cecilia asked with undisguised hostility. "Are you not aware of your reputation?"

"I suppose I've made quite the name for myself," Janis conceded without a hint of shame.

He didn't appear to be afraid of Dante. On the contrary, he was perfectly at ease as he glanced around before narrowing his eyes as he took stock of the situation.

"I see I'm surrounded. That explains why we still haven't gotten our teas."

The staff and the other customers were all watching Cecilia and Janis. They looked alert, ready to spring into action.

"I didn't even notice when the swap took place, I must admit," Janis added with a smile, evidently finding it all rather amusing.

A short-haired woman wearing no-nonsense trousers and shirt appeared next to their table. She crossed her arms. This finally seemed to throw Janis a little.

"How long has it been? New haircut, I see. It suits your pretty face, even with the scars."

"You still think women exist purely to have their looks rated by you, pig?"

It was Marlin Sweeney, the leader of the now-disbanded assassins' syndicate, Heimat, who'd raised Dante. Her gaze fell briefly on Cecilia before she focused her full attention on Janis again.

"Oh, but I was trying to compliment you."

"I don't want your compliments, so save yourself the effort."

"Some people just can't be pleased," Janis shrugged. Then he raised his hands in a gesture of surrender. "I'm gravely outnumbered, and I'm guessing you'd be quite skilled at evading my touch."

"We won't let you put your hands on anyone."

"So what happens now? Are you going to capture me? Kill me? Or do you have something even more nasty in mind?"

Cecilia answered him.

"Nobody is getting killed. You won't be hurt, but you'll have to answer some questions and hand over the Dirk of Destiny. You'll be coming with me to the royal palace, too."

"You want me to see the king? Does this mean you're going to get me deported?"

"..."

"That would be quite the inconvenience for me. I wasn't planning on going home so soon," he said without appearing bothered at all. "Cecil, you asked me earlier if I wasn't aware of my reputation. I could throw that question right back at you."

"Huh?"

"Did you think I wouldn't have taken precautions before meeting you?"

Janis clapped his hands over his head and in an instant, dark miasma started wafting into the café from the surrounding area. Someone screamed.

"What the—"

"Boss! The civilians we had put to sleep have woken up, and they're possessed!"

"The street vendors are possessed, too!"

"Even the florist has been affected!"

"You've got to be kidding me!"

Marlin immediately began issuing orders to her panicked

underlings. Janis' calm voice stood out against this busy backdrop of noise.

"I'm sorry I didn't tell you I could also time the germination of the Obstruction seeds."

"What…?"

"There are ten Obstructions here right now. Do you think Marlin and her subordinates can subdue them without any casualties?"

They could hear fighting and more screaming. Shaking with rage, Cecilia was about to say something to Janis when someone called out to him. She turned and saw three knives flying in her direction. Dante pulled her back before she could react, kicking the table up into the air. The blades burrowed into the wooden surface.

"I'll see you some other time, Cecil. Bye!"

Cecilia looked up to find Janis sitting on a horse behind the long-haired, mean-eyed bodyguard she'd seen at the Advent festival. He must have thrown the knives at her. She watched them ride away at full speed, feeling disoriented and powerless.

It took half an hour to get the incident under control. Eins and Zwei had heard the commotion and came running to join Marlin and her people. In the end, nobody died, and only a few people suffered minor injuries. Cecilia asked the twins to report what had happened while she stayed behind to thank Dante.

"I owe you big time for this, Dante. Are you okay? Did you get hurt?"

"Of course not, don't be silly. I almost didn't make it in time. I went to get Marlin and her team as an extra precaution, so it took a bit longer than expected."

Cecilia had asked Dante for help before leaving with Eins and Zwei to meet Janis. Finding him sitting in an empty classroom, she'd hastily explained the situation without mentioning the Dirk of

Destiny, and he agreed to secretly escort her. Eins and Zwei weren't aware of his true identity, so Cecilia couldn't tell them that they would have a bodyguard with them on that escapade.

"Don't worry, you didn't miss anything! I thought it'd be just you following us, but it sure helped to have the extra pairs of hands! And it was nice to see Marlin again."

"Well, I'm happy to hear that."

"Oh, you're here!" Cecilia exclaimed joyously, seeing Marlin reappear beside Dante.

She looked at Cecilia as warmly as one would a sister.

"It's lovely to see you, Marlin. Thank you so much for your help!"

"Hey, I owed you one for saving my skin last time. So now we're even." She paused briefly before adding, "Although your skin may be worth more than mine, heh. On a different note, I heard from Dante that you were attending the academy pretending to be a boy, but it's wild seeing you like this. You've got the craziest ideas, don't you? That goes for having a chat with Janis, too…"

"Ha-ha…"

"If I hadn't seen it myself, I wouldn't have believed that a human could control Obstructions. You knew about this and still went out to find him?"

Marlin gave her a serious look. She must have overheard most of Cecilia's conversation with Janis.

"Kind of…" She gave a vague answer.

Marlin let out a loud sigh.

"Goodness, girl. Being reckless is one thing, but what you seem to have no self-preservation instinct whatsoever! You'd better do something about that before your luck runs out."

"What are you getting so worked up about, Marlin? No one was badly hurt, so all's well that ends well, no?"

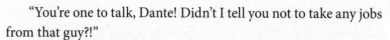

"You're one to talk, Dante! Didn't I tell you not to take any jobs from that guy?!"

"Let go, you're hurting me!"

Marlin pulled Dante by his ear. Cecilia thought Dante had made a good point and didn't deserve to be reprimanded, but based on the fact he wasn't resisting, he probably felt guilty over having worked for Janis against Marlin's advice. Cecilia raised her hand to get their attention.

"By 'taking jobs,' do you mean when Janis hired Dante to assassinate Oscar?"

"You're well-informed. Yes, precisely."

Neither Marlin nor Dante had originally accepted Janis' request. It was another member of Heimat who'd lost to Janis in a gamble and owed him a favor. The prince had been vague on the nature of the job, revealing only that the target was a noble. When it later transpired that the person Janis wanted killed was a royal, Marlin intervened to annul the contract. Janis then requested that Heimat pay him a fine for breaking the deal, a fee so exorbitantly high that it would have put the organization out of business.

"We could've found a loophole to get out of paying him, but trust is even more important for groups like us than for above board organizations. Bad reviews can be devastating for an assassination business. So, I was going to get that money somehow, but Dante here took it upon himself to save us from financial ruin by fulfilling the request all by himself."

"If you ended up paying, the other members would have ganged up on poor Jan and killed him."

"He'd have brought it upon himself by accepting that shady request. We used to have quite a few short-tempered members back in the day."

Marlin explained this all like it was no big deal. She and Dante had dealt with death on a regular basis, so talking about one of their companions narrowly escaping with his life didn't arouse strong emotions in them, but Cecilia found it quite uncomfortable to listen to.

"So you took that request to save your friend, Dante?"

"Yup! I didn't end up fulfilling it, though!"

"And what happened to Jan? Is he okay?"

"He's fine, though now he's responsible for all our menial labor," replied Marlin.

Cecilia followed the woman's sharp gaze to a scrawny-looking man being ordered around. Was that Jan?

"The clique who wanted to kill him got wiped out during that mess when we kidnapped you. He's one lucky bastard."

"Then what about the fine you were obligated to pay?"

"Heimat got disbanded, so all its debts are invalid. I've had to start from scratch again, but at least that whole deal with Janis won't be a blot on our rep." Marlin smiled broadly, a cunning look on her face, which disappeared after a moment. "Oh, by the way." She fished a piece of paper out of her pocket. "I've got something for you."

"What's this…? A map?"

"See the tavern marked on it? If you need anything from us in future, you can get in touch by leaving a letter with the barkeep."

"Um…"

"Don't worry about money. You owe us nothing for today, since it was a rather poor showing anyway. And your next request is on the house, too, so don't be shy."

"Really? Gosh, thanks so much!"

Cecilia clutched the map as though it were an extremely precious item. Marlin reached out and tousled her hair, just like Dante would sometimes do.

"Needless to say, I'll pretend I hadn't overheard anything today, but seriously, be careful. Janis is a nasty piece of work. If you're going to contact him again, make sure to keep your distance and always have someone with you. Okay?"

"Okay, I'll be careful!"

Marlin smiled at Cecilia's docile reply.

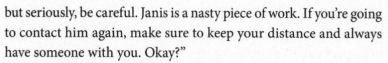

Little did Oscar know that the next day would start on a horrible note that crushed his spirits.

"I must have misheard you. Say that again?"

"I saved Cecilia from Prince Janis yesterday."

"You did WHAT?"

"How many times do I need to repeat myself? I saved Cecilia. From Janis. She asked for my help."

He'd only just entered the classroom and sat at his desk when Dante came out with that shocker. Outside, the sky was blue and the school was bathed in sunshine, but dark clouds seemed to have gathered over Oscar.

He and Dante were the only students in the classroom, both having arrived fairly early. Oscar rubbed his forehead and closed his eyes, as if assailed by a sudden headache.

"It wasn't related to that incident with Obstructions showing up in the city center, was it?" he asked in a faltering voice.

"Sure was!"

Dante's cheerful reply sent Oscar plunging into the depths of depression. He'd only just arrived, but all he wanted now was to go home.

Oscar had, of course, been notified of Obstructions manifesting in the city the previous day. According to the report, the situation was brought under control thanks to the efforts of some knights and brave civilians who happened to be on the scene. He had no reason to suspect Cecilia's involvement.

I thought she rarely ventured off campus...

If it were Jade, Dante, or Eins and Zwei, it wouldn't surprise him. They often hung out in the city after school.

Oscar propped his elbows on the table, interlaced his fingers, and rested his forehead on the back of his hands. Then he sighed deeply.

"Something wrong?"

Oscar wondered whether his friend was clueless or just playing dumb.

"I feel like I'm about to lose my mind from an overwhelming mix of powerlessness, annoyance, jealousy, and relief."

"Wow, your inner life is so complex!" Dante chuckled with zero sympathy.

Normally, Oscar was comfortable with Dante's unreserved attitude toward him, but on this occasion, it only irked him.

"Jealousy and relief make sense, but what are you angry about?"

"Her always being so reckless."

"Ah, right. Hmm. Well, that's just Cecil for you, though."

Dante was absolutely right. Cecil/Cecilia was impulsive by nature, and nothing could change that. The real reason Oscar was angry was that he could never stop worrying about something happening to her.

He lifted his head and looked at Dante, who was standing next to him.

"Judging from how lightly you're treating this, I assume she didn't get hurt?"

"Oh, rest assured there's not a scratch on her. Or on me, thank you for asking."

"I wasn't worried about you, Dante."

"Oh, so you don't care what happens to me, is that it? How cold."

"I'm not cold."

"Yes, you are!"

Dante was pretending to be offended, but had Oscar asked if he was all right, he would have taken issue with that, too. He'd probably say something along the lines of, "Do you need to ask? Do you not trust in my skills?" At any rate, it was true that Oscar never worried about Dante. He knew the assassin could take care of himself and wriggle out of any perilous situation.

Cecilia, though, was nothing like him.

She hadn't been trained as an assassin. She kept brushing against death, surviving only thanks to a combination of extreme willpower, motivation, and sheer luck. How could Oscar not feel anxious about her luck eventually running out?

But I know her too well by now to understand that patience and caution are alien concepts to her...

In the twelve years when Oscar hadn't able to see Cecilia, he believed her to be an almost ephemeral being, fragile and living in total seclusion from the world. He wouldn't have guessed that she actually was a headstrong, boisterous girl. Kind of a tomboy...in fact, she went so far beyond being a tomboy that she was actually passing herself off as a boy at school.

Staring at the ceiling, Dante perched on Oscar's desk and spoke to him.

"Cecil and Prince Janis seemed to have a conflict of interest of some sort."

"Huh?"

"I didn't quite follow their conversation, but it was something to do with an item they referred to as the Dirk of Destiny."

"The Dirk of Destiny…?" Oscar repeated, making a thoughtful expression.

"You know what it is?" Dante's eyes flashed with curiosity.

"Isn't that the dagger from the legend? It's supposedly real, but nobody has actually seen it. From what I've heard, it doesn't have any special powers. It's merely an ornamental knife."

"I wonder why Cecilia and that bastard were interested in it?"

"How would I know?!"

Too late, Oscar realized that he'd openly admitted to having no clue as to what his fiancée was up to. He pressed his hand against his chest as if he'd been stabbed in the heart. He didn't know why Cecilia wanted some mythical dagger. She wouldn't even tell him why she was pretending to be a boy—in fact, she was under the impression that he was still being duped by her disguise. She never confided in him about anything.

"Maybe Gilbert does. Why don't you ask him? Oh… Were you trying to punch me just now?"

"Curse you!"

"Jealousy is such an ugly feeling."

"You're really asking for it now."

Truth be told, though, he could forgive Dante, and even Gilbert, for teasing him. They were annoying, but their snide remarks didn't make him angry. Most of the time.

"By the way, I have one more thing to report. It seems that Prince Janis can control Obstructions. I was standing too far away to hear much of what he and Cecilia were talking about, but they mentioned Eins and Zwei's mother. I'm guessing Janis had something to do with her murder."

"I see…"

"You don't seem surprised."

"It would explain what happened on Advent Day."

Oscar had his suspicions even back then. When Janis had told them that the Holy Maiden seemed to be in trouble, he looked like he knew exactly what was going on. As if he was behind it all. If he could summon Obstructions at will, the pieces of the puzzle would all fall in place.

"Will you be reporting it to the king?"

"Yes, but I highly doubt he can take action against Janis."

"I guess even the king can't do much about another nation's prince."

"There's that, yes, but the problem here is that we have no proof. Father would likely scold me for giving credence to foolish rumors."

"Ah. I guess it is kind of hard to believe."

"Also, in Janis' case, trying to solve anything via the diplomatic route may be futile. We should capture him, if possible. He has entered our country illegally, so it would be perfectly justifiable."

That was easier said than done. Janis was one slippery customer, and even if they did succeed at capturing him, he would undoubtedly stir up more trouble. Oscar explained this to Dante, ending his mini lecture with a heavy sigh.

"Janis is a real pain in the neck, hmm?"

"...I wasn't thinking about him just now. It's not fair, Dante. Why did she have to ask you for help? Why not me? I could have kept her safe, too. She doesn't even need to tell me who she really is—I'd do it for Cecil."

"Oh no! You're jealous of me?"

You could almost HEAR a vein pop out on Oscar's forehead.

"Why do I even put up with you?!" he yelled, pinching Dante's cheek and twisting it painfully.

"I was only joking!" Dante chuckled. "Anyway, weren't you busy yesterday? At the palace?"

"Yes..."

"Then how could you expect Cecilia to find you on short notice and ask you to come along? And even if you were at hand, I don't think she'd want you to get anywhere near the guy who wants you dead so much he even hired an assassin for the job."

"I hadn't thought about that."

"Well, there you have it."

Oscar had wanted to be there for Cecilia to protect her, but she hadn't mentioned anything to him to keep HIM safe? Feeling pathetic, Oscar slumped back in his chair with a glum look on his face.

For the rest of the morning, Oscar was too deflated to focus on anything. He did have a lot on his to-do list, which only kept growing longer, but he just couldn't think. He managed to accomplish some things in a purely robotic way, his mind elsewhere the entire time. And even though he was aware of it, there was nothing he could do to shake off the paralyzing dejection.

It was lunchtime. Oscar was making his way down a hallway, the mess of emotions in his head crystallizing into self-loathing.

There's no reason it should bother me, so why does it affect me so much?

He decided to confront his feelings and admit to himself that for the past few months—since he'd found out who Cecil really was—he'd been out of sorts.

If I want her to rely on me, maybe I should tell her that I know it's her...

But then he remembered Gilbert warning him last summer holiday that his sister would flee to another country if she realized that Oscar knew her secret. The thought of her doing that terrified him.

Gilbert said it wouldn't make a difference to him, since he'd just go with her, but Oscar couldn't leave.

"What reason would she have to flee the country anyway?" he muttered absent-mindedly.

She was fine with Dante knowing her secret. Why not him? He couldn't puzzle this out.

She doesn't despise me. To the best of my knowledge, I've never done anything that might make her afraid of me...

He was so preoccupied that he stopped walking and froze in the middle of the hallway. There wasn't another student in sight, so everyone else must have already moved on to lunch.

I wish she'd ask me for help at least once...

"Oscar! Heeelp!"

"Huh?"

At first, he thought he'd imagined it, that his tired mind was playing tricks on him. Nevertheless, he turned toward the voice and saw his panicked fiancée running toward him so fast that it was a miracle her short, honey-blond wig stayed on her head. When she got to him, she grabbed his hands and pleaded, looking as if she might burst into tears:

"Hide me!"

"Wait, what's going on?"

But Cecilia had no time to explain. She stepped behind Oscar and moved him slightly, so that he stood in between the wall and a pillar. Thanks to their difference in size, she was thus perfectly concealed.

A moment later, they heard footsteps. A few people were running toward them.

"Where is he?!"

"You can't run from responsibility!"

"Reap what you sowed!"

Three angry guys ran past Oscar. Each nodded in greeting as they went by, but they didn't notice that there was someone standing behind the prince, so they didn't stop.

Cecilia finally poked out her face from behind Oscar a short while after they disappeared. She had been standing behind him with her arms raised in front of her face. Now she was cautiously peeking out from between them, looking like a frightened bunny. Even dressed like a guy, his fiancée was unbearably cute.

Reassured that the danger had passed, Cecilia dropped her arms and flashed a bright smile at Oscar.

"Thanks so much! You saved my skin!"

"What have you done this time?"

She laughed awkwardly at his exasperated question.

"I haven't done anything, but this girl told me she'd fallen in love with me, and it just so happened that she was already engaged to someone..."

"Ah. So her fiancé and his friends wanted to punish you for meddling with her?"

That would make it the third time this month, as far as Oscar was aware. Girls kept falling for the academy's "prince" left and right.

"No, this time it's a bit different..."

"Oh?"

"The fiancé wants me to accept her proposal."

"He what?" Oscar wasn't sure he'd heard that right.

"Her fiancé said he knew that she had the hots for me, and he wants me to marry her because I owe it to her for stealing her heart, apparently? He got really pushy about that and said he wouldn't forgive me if I hurt her feelings..."

"I...see..."

"The ex-fiancés of Luise and Irina overheard him pestering me, and the next thing I knew, they started trying to convince me that the girls they're engaged to are way cuter than Agnes, and I should marry one of them instead."

That was some twisted love. On the one hand, it was nice that the guys respected the feelings of the girls they were engaged to, but trying to pressure their rival into marrying them sounded crazy to Oscar.

Would that really be a satisfying outcome for them?

What would he do in their place? If Cecilia developed feelings for another man?

My stomach hurts...

Imagining it was enough to make him feel physically ill. He didn't think he'd genuinely want to help Cecilia get together with another man, even if she were head over heels for him.

"Anyhow! Thanks for the help, Oscar!"

"Sure..."

"You're so tall, so it was easy for me to hide behind you!"

The difference in their height was quite striking. Oscar was more than a head taller, and wider in the shoulders, too. Cecilia had told him she was training to get stronger, but her build was so slight that she looked delicate and precious, especially next to him.

She stepped out from the gap between the wall and the pillar and stood in front of Oscar. He glanced down at her.

"By the way, I heard about yesterday from Dante."

"Ah, okay."

"You've got to stop doing crazy things like that. It stressed me out so much to hear about your escapade. You should always come to me first if you—"

"Stop! No more lectures!"

"Ngh..."

Cecilia pressed her hands against his lips, as if to physically stop the words from coming out of his mouth. When he went quiet without putting up a fight, she gave him a tearful look again and explained:

"Gilbert was so, so mad at me when I got back yesterday! I have reflected on my actions, I promise you I have! Please don't be mad at me! If anything, I need some TLC after that ordeal!"

TLC?

Oscar was baffled. What exactly did she want him to do? He pondered that for a moment before placing his right hand on Cecilia's head.

"Er... It must have been hard for you. Glad you made it back in one piece."

"Huh?" Cecilia was confused by the sudden head pats.

"Was that not right either?"

"No, but... I wasn't expecting you to actually be kind to me!"

"I just did as you requested."

"I guess so...mmm," she said, still seeming somewhat thrown.

He kept stroking her hair in silence for a minute or two.

"You have really big hands, Oscar."

"They only look that way next to yours."

"Gil and Dante's hands are also bigger than mine... I guess that's just one of the differences..."

Between girls and boys? Oscar could only guess at her unfinished sentence. He kept stroking her hair.

"It was a nightmare yesterday! Eins and Zwei picked the worst possible day to spring their plan. Gil was away."

"That's rough..." Oscar nodded, feeling a pang of jealousy.

"And you were off somewhere, too!"

"Oh? You tried to find me?"

"Yeah! After talking to the Machiases, I ran over to your

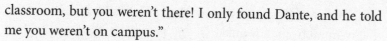

classroom, but you weren't there! I only found Dante, and he told me you weren't on campus."

Oscar looked at her incredulously.

"So it wasn't Dante you originally wanted to ask for help? I was your first choice?" he ventured.

"Yup! I knew that I wouldn't be able to do much to help Eins and Zwei on my own. I thought I might even just get in the way more than anything. But you're a prince, like Janis, so you should be able to take him, right?"

"Wait, so you weren't trying to protect me?"

"Er... What?"

"You didn't decide to keep me out of this to keep me safe from Janis?"

Cecilia gaped at him. It was obvious that it hadn't occurred to her.

"Oh... Oooh! You shouldn't bring along an assassination attempt target to a meeting with the dude who hired the hitman... Gosh, I'm so sorry, Oscar. I was really careless!"

"I didn't mean to say you were..."

"Excuses, excuses, I know, but I think it didn't cross my mind because I was so sure you'd be fine no matter what happened," she carried on apologetically. "You wouldn't lose to the likes of Janis! You're a good guy, diligent and earnest, and righteous to boot!"

"..."

"I hadn't forgotten that he tried to kill you, but it seemed kind of irrelevant to me because I don't see you losing to him, ever!"

Cecilia followed her assertion with an embarrassed chuckle. That laugh, and her words, melted the icy self-doubt which had been tormenting Oscar. She did see him as someone to rely on. It made him happy.

"Oh, but if you'd rather steer clear of Janis, I'll be sure to keep that in mind from now on!"

"No, I don't mind."

"You sure?"

"Yeah. I won't lose to him, ever," he repeated her words playfully.

Cecilia's face lit up with a smile.

"Of course not! He's got nothing on you!"

She took his words at face value with childlike naïveté. Her unshakable belief in him made Oscar happy, but also a little embarrassed, so while he smiled involuntarily back at her, it was somewhat uneasy. Hoping to hide how self-conscious he was feeling, he patted Cecilia on the back and changed the subject.

"Let's not stand around in the hallway all lunchtime long, or else we won't get to eat."

"Oops, I totally forgot! Gil must be getting fed up with waiting for me!"

Then she took Oscar's hand.

"Come along!"

"Is that okay?"

"Sure it is! Lean and Huey will be there as well! And Jade said he'd come! If we see Dante on the way, let's invite him to have lunch with us too!"

She wanted to check if Eins and Zwei were still in their classroom. Thus dragged along, Oscar smiled wryly.

Main roads chock-full of people. Decorated trees. Stalls with slanted roofs, adorned with lanterns with green and red ribbons, that filled the square where children would ordinarily be playing. Metal arches that had been erected on the streets specifically for this occasion leading to the site of festivities, which also sported vividly colored lanterns.

The chilly air turned breath into white puffs and reddened everyone's cheeks. It was December. After the Halloween event, this world's version of Christmas followed.

"Let's enjoy Nativity!" Lean exclaimed enthusiastically.

They were at Lean's old home, the Cigogne Orphanage. The open area where a stage had been built for her play a few months back now featured three pop-up booths.

The Nativity was another major festival, this time celebrating the birth of Lumiel, the goddess' and Ian's baby. A street fair called the Naissance Market was held in the city from December until January as part of the Nativity celebrations. It was the biggest of its kind in the country, and even people who weren't merchants by trade opened up small booths or sold handmade goods out of their houses. Traders from other towns also arrived in droves to take advantage of this special event.

The city was bustling like it had been during Advent, but the atmosphere of Nativity was quite different from then since it was more of a secular celebration. The Church of Caritade was hands-off with the festivities—instead, it was the common folk who took the initiative to hold a big, exciting event before the quiet winter days ahead.

The plaza in front of the orphanage was mostly empty, save for a wooden frame. Cecilia joined the resident children to help them with preparations for the market. She was carrying a wooden crate.

"Does it go here?"

"Yes! If you could just put it under that table, that'll be fine!" replied Lean.

The nuns had designated Lean as the person in charge of their local market. She was giving instructions to the children and Cecilia with a sketch of the layout in hand.

"This is the second time I'm amazed by how seriously this city takes festivals."

"Wait, you've never been here for the Nativity?"

"Nope. I was always back at my family's residence this time of year."

Everything was a big production in the capital, it seemed. Meanwhile, some other parts of the country didn't celebrate Nativity at all.

"And what did you do last year?"

"Huh?" Cecilia wasn't sure what Lean was asking about.

"Were you already Cecil during last year's Nativity? Has it been a year yet since you assumed this fake persona?"

"Ah, no. I wasn't actually attending classes back then."

"Why not?"

"Gil was worried about me being at the academy all on my own. He asked me to wait until he could enroll, too."

"So he's always been overprotective of you."

"I didn't mind, though. I wanted to get a good idea of what the academy was like before making my first appearance as Cecil. I had private tutors at home, so I didn't fall behind."

In retrospect, it hadn't been the smartest strategy. A stunningly handsome boy joining in the middle of the academic year was bound to become the focus of attention. Owing to that, she'd earned herself the title of Vleugel Academy's prince barely a month out from when she started attending school as Cecil.

"I bet Gilbert didn't see it coming that you'd become the campus heartthrob instead of keeping a low profile."

"Yeah… He interrogated me about how it came to that…"

Cecilia stared into the distance with a traumatized look in her eyes. That wasn't a memory she wanted to revisit.

"That ship has sailed, but didn't you consider about giving the academy a miss entirely? You wouldn't have had to take part in the Selection Ceremony for sure."

"Oh, that was my plan initially, but then I got thinking, what if the heroine fails to get any Artifacts?"

In her past life as Hiyono, Cecilia hadn't seen what happened in that ending. To be more precise, she didn't even know if an ending like that existed in the game, and what it might entail for the villainess of the story. Spending an entire year without knowing anything about how the situation was progressing would have been agonizing for her, so she'd ultimately ended up enrolling in the academy to follow the developments and intervene if needed.

"I think I made the right call," Cecilia said, looking pointedly at Lean.

Lean couldn't hold her gaze.

"Don't blame me for this situation. I don't want to become a Holy Maiden, either. Besides, if Prince Janis is telling the truth, it seems like we won't need Holy Maidens after all, since it's the Church of Caritade who's responsible for the Obstructions' appearance."

"He could be lying."

Cecilia had briefed Lean, Grace, and Gilbert about her conversation with Janis. They had come to the conclusion that Janis' explanation for the Obstructions should be ignored for the time being. He might have made the story up to manipulate them into doing something advantageous for him. Also, Janis said that there was probably nobody left even at the Church who knew how the system worked. The clergy could be sowing the seeds without realizing what they were doing or that those seeds might grow into Obstructions.

"Also, Gil said something pretty disturbing…"

"Yeah?"

"That if this system is set up so that the seeds will stop germinating once the new Holy Maiden has been determined, which prevents new Obstructions from manifesting, then the Obstructions will…keep appearing in the event a Maiden isn't chosen."

In which case, they would really need a new Holy Maiden, or the item that could stop the Obstructions forever, which was currently in Janis' possession.

"We really shouldn't be spending our time on festival stuff in this situation…"

"But you haven't made any progress in the last two weeks anyway."

"Well, yeah. Janis has a whole bunch of aliases, so even Gil hasn't been able to track him down. Janis said he'd see me again some other time, so I thought he'd try to contact me, but he hasn't so far."

"What a pity that big baddie Janis hasn't come looking for you…"

Lean rolled her eyes, but when Cecilia gave her a crestfallen look, she patted her shoulders encouragingly.

"Forget about that for now, and focus your efforts on helping me out here! You're not going back home for the winter break, are you?"

"No. It's best I stay away to keep my parents safe."

On the odd chance that Janis did come see her, she didn't want her family to be nearby. Cecilia would never be able to forgive herself if they got embroiled in this risky business.

"That means Gil's staying here too, right? Your mom and dad are going to miss you guys."

"Nah, they'll be fine! We did go home for the summer break, and we saw each other during Advent, too. In their last letter, they told me they'd send me something soon. My bets are on Becky's scones! You're invited for tea when they arrive."

"I'll come if I'm feeling up to it," Lean replied standoffishly.

Despite appearances, Lean was quite sociable by nature and had never passed up an invitation for tea and snacks before, so Cecilia smiled, assured that her friend would come. Then she picked up a crate from a wheelbarrow and carried it toward the stall where she'd dropped off the other one earlier.

"Gosh, this is really heavy. Is it full of bricks or what?"

"Don't—"

But it was too late. Cecilia had already lifted the lid to peek inside.

"Books? No, wait…"

"Heh-heh… Anyone's welcome to set up their own stall at the market, after all."

The crate was stuffed full of Madame Neal's novels. Tales of boys in love with other boys—not the sort of publication you'd normally find being sold outside an orphanage. The spines were a different color from Lean's earlier works. Could it be that...she'd written a third volume of that story with characters based on Oscar and Cecil?

Cecilia picked up one of the volumes with shaking hands.

"I'm very satisfied with how this one turned out! And guess what! It's set during Nativity!" Lean spoke fast with enthusiasm.

"You matched it to the real-world timing again, huh..."

"In this volume, Ciel and a prince from a neighboring country—another top—engage in many action-packed battles, all revolving around Oran, the bottom."

"Uh..."

A prince from a neighboring country? No way... Could Lean have modelled that character after Janis? The man who wanted her dead, the guy whose guts she should hate?

"Of course, the story ends with Ciel slaying the prince! Like this!"

Lean mimed cutting a foe down with a sword. So she did hold a grudge against Janis, and her way of processing these negative emotions was to kill him off in her novel. Classic Lean.

She put her hands on her hips.

"And I'm planning on trying something more ambitious in future if it sells well."

"More ambitious? Like what?"

"Like turning the Naissance Market into a comic market."

"Right, I don't want to play any part in that!"

Her friend was planning to establish manga fandom in this alternate universe. This seemed plain wrong to Cecilia. She covered her ears, but Lean continued, undeterred.

"The thing is, self-publishing is not a commonly understood concept in this world. Yet. I've been talking with Jade about whether we could guide aspiring artists through the process, but the costs of printing are prohibitive to most..."

Lean didn't want comic-making to be a hobby accessible only to the rich, and it sounded like she already had some ideas for how to address that. She seemed more terrifyingly unstoppable than Prince Janis to Cecilia. Her friend was going to corrupt this world.

"Oh, hello!" came a clear, sweet voice.

They turned to see a familiar bespectacled lady with cute freckles. She was blushing.

"Lord Cecil! And Lady Lean!"

"Hello, Elza!" Cecilia called out cheerfully when Elza hurried over to them.

They noticed that the abbess had brought several nuns with her.

"What brings you here?"

"The Holy Maiden has sent us out to visit all orphanages and offer prayers in her stead. Her recent poor health is preventing her from leaving the shrine."

Elza smiled, but there was a hint of worry in her eyes. Then she noticed the crates next to Lean and Cecilia.

"You're busy with preparations for the market? Oh, isn't that...?"

She widened her eyes, then snatched a pale green book out of Cecilia's hands.

"H-hey!"

"A new novel by Madame Neal?!"

Her eyes were sparkling with excitement. Taken aback by Elza's lack of reserve, Cecilia raised her hand to ask a question.

"Um...so you've heard about Madame Neal?"

"Have I heard about her? I read all her stories! Her books are very popular with the nuns, you know. She opened my eyes to the delights of bittersweet love between young men!" she spoke with passion.

Was it really all right for nuns, who had vowed to live out their lives in chastity, to read steamy gay romances? Then again, maybe

99

it wasn't such a big deal. There was no harm in enjoying fiction, right?

"How did you get your hands on this new release before I even heard about it?! I'm so happy to meet fellow fans of Madame Neal, though! I feel instantly closer to you! What did you think of the previous volume? Wasn't Ciel so cute, burning with jealousy over his crush?"

Elza swayed and gestured excitedly, unaware that she was talking to the author herself and the person Ciel was modeled on. She gushed with admiration over Lean's books for about five minutes without letting anyone else get a word in before regaining control over herself.

"Oh, sorry. I got overexcited." She cleared her throat and straightened her clothes. "I'll be minding a stall at the Naissance Market in the big plaza, collecting donations. Come say hello if you find yourself in the area."

She then said good-bye and left with her nuns for the church beside the orphanage. Sisters who ran the orphanage gathered up the children and headed there, too, presumably to pray together.

"Elza's quite the character."

"Yeah. I had this image in my head of all clerics being formal and restrained, but she's nothing like it."

"She used to be quite somber, actually," interjected one of the nuns, who they only now realized had stayed behind. She had chestnut hair, and her face looked familiar…

That's the lady we ran into ran into when we were searching for the Dirk of Destiny!

They'd given her and her patrol partner quite the scare back then.

"Really?" asked Lean, tilting her head to the side.

The nun lowered her voice.

"Oh yes. She used to be really quiet and kept to herself. Her

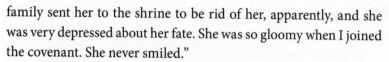

family sent her to the shrine to be rid of her, apparently, and she was very depressed about her fate. She was so gloomy when I joined the covenant. She never smiled."

"But then she started reading Madame Neal's books and changed immensely!"

"That's right!"

Several other nuns had appeared around them, joining the conversation.

"We all enjoy Madame Neal's stories, but they've become the center of Elza's world!"

"She pores over them over and over again."

"The copies we have at the shrine are worn out from her reading them so much."

"Oh, wow," Cecilia commented, not really sure what else to say.

It wasn't a clear-cut good outcome from Cecilia's point of view. A novel had helped a woman find her inner light again—that sounded great, sure. But this book just so happened to be a BL fantasy starring a character based on her.

"It's, um, it's good she's getting so much out of them, I guess," she managed in the end.

"Yes, it is!" the nuns replied in unison.

They hadn't gathered around Cecilia and Lean to talk about Elza, though. Their flushed cheeks and sparkling eyes were a dead giveaway that they longed to be in the company of Cecil.

"What's keeping you?! Come over here!" Elza called out to them from outside the church.

"Coming!" they replied cheerfully and trotted over to where the abbess was waiting.

"So here's the deal. Let's have a tea party before the winter break!" said Cecilia.

It was two days after their unexpected encounter with Elza. Cecilia was in the lounge with the whole gang, which included even Eins, Zwei, Mordred, and Grace this time.

Huey eyed the cheery Cecilia suspiciously.

"And why are we doing this now?"

"Um, because I just got this care package from my mom!"

She stepped to the side, revealing a pile of wooden boxes. They were stacked up to Cecilia's height in two rows.

"Whoa. You could open a store," said Jade in astonishment.

"My mom went a bit overboard when I wrote to her that I wouldn't be coming home for the winter break. There are cakes and snacks that don't keep very well, so I'd appreciate your help getting through them!"

Lucinda Sylvie's boundless love for her daughter had manifested in physical form as a bounty of food. There were fresh desserts, bucket-loads of tea leaves, chocolates from a patisserie Cecilia liked, and a mountain of Becky's scones. Gilbert wasn't planning on going home either, so it was meant for both of them, but there was no way two people could eat so much before it went bad.

"Does your mom not know that the canteen's still open over the break? And that you can cook at the dorm, too?"

"She's plenty aware, but she worries about me having enough to eat anyway..."

That's why she had them stay at the family residence during the summer break, but of course Jade couldn't know that.

Cecilia pressed her palms together imploringly.

"Anyway, this is how things are! Please help me eat this delicious food, or most of it will go to waste!"

"I can help with that," offered Eins.

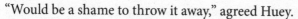

"Would be a shame to throw it away," agreed Huey.

"Wow, that's quite a selection!"

"There are even smoked meats! Is this wild boar? And venison?"

Jade and Zwei were already checking the contents of the boxes.

"Yup. My dad's gotten into hunting recently."

"Smoked meats? Score! You guys wait here, and I'll be right back with something that goes reeeally well with charcuterie!" Dante got up and headed out of the lounge.

"Don't bring anything bizarre!" Gilbert called after him.

"Sure, sure!" Dante replied without paying him much attention.

Lean and Oscar went over to take a look inside the boxes too.

"I just can't believe how much food your mom sent you…"

"This is more than all of us can finish in a day…or two…"

"If there's anything you want, you're welcome to take some home!"

"Is it okay if I take some food to the orphanage?"

"Yeah, sure! I can even help you with that!"

"I'm willing to help, too," volunteered Oscar.

"And me!" Jade raised his hand.

"You can count me in as well," Zwei said with a shy smile.

The other guys were also willing to help out with delivering some of the food to the orphanage.

"I'd like to know why you invited us, too?" Mordred's calm voice cut through the din of the excited voices in the lounge.

Grace nodded as if to say she was wondering about that as well. The two stood out in the group of students.

"Because I've got gifts for the both of you!" said Cecilia, rummaging through a bag.

"What's the occasion?"

"Well, you didn't get to join us on the trip to the shrine, so I figured I'd at least buy you something while we were there!"

"Oh. That's very thoughtful."

She handed them two little bottles filled with a transparent liquid that looked like oil. Mordred raised an eyebrow and lifted his bottle up to the light to examine it.

"What's this?"

"Cologne. Torche is famous for lilac flowers and lilac-scented products, like cologne and candles. Oh, I've got another one for Emily. With a slightly different scent."

"It smells lovely," Grace said with a smile, sniffing the contents of her bottle of perfume.

Cecilia gave Mordred the bottle for Emily.

"Thank you kindly for bringing back a gift not only for me, but for Emily as well. At her age, I imagine she'll be thrilled to get foreign perfume."

"Your choice of gifts just screams Vleugel Prince, Cecil," teased Eins.

"Rare perfume's what you'd normally use for wooing girls, hmm?" Zwei joined in.

Cecilia had actually given them cologne as well.

"Cecil knows what ladies like!"

"You picked subtle and refined scents like a perfume connoisseur."

"Ha-ha…"

Cecilia laughed awkwardly, glad that they had assumed she was knowledgeable about perfume because she was the school's famous flirt, and not because she was, in fact, a girl.

"Gilbert's not going home for the winter break either, huh? If you guys are staying here, then so am I. My folks would just force me to help out with the business," Jade said, changing the subject.

He'd picked out his favorite foods from the boxes and did a big stretch.

"Great! The more friends staying, the better!" replied Dante, who'd just returned to the lounge.

"Wait, you're staying, too?"

"Yeah. No point in me going back home."

"Why? Did you fall out with your parents? Nothing but bad vibes at home?"

"Something like that."

Dante wasn't really an aristocrat. He'd bought his title and a false identity from the Hamptons, a noble family who'd left the country to start a new life elsewhere. Their old residence probably still existed, but nobody lived there anymore, and without anyone to maintain the place, it might have already turned into an inhabitable ruin.

Oscar, who was well-aware of Dante's situation, crossed his arms.

"Why don't you stay at my home, as I suggested before? We have no shortage of guest rooms."

"That's so nice of you to offer, but it's the royal palace we're talking about, right? I could never feel relaxed there. With your family around, I would need to get official permission just to go on a casual outing with you. Besides, what is there to do at the palace anyway?"

"If so many of you are staying on campus, maybe I will, too," Lean said in her fake demure girl voice. "There isn't much for me to do at home, and I'd much rather be with Huey!"

"Hey, cut it out," Huey complained when she clung to him in a tight embrace, doing a poor job of hiding his delight.

Jade shifted in his seat, leaning closer to him.

"You're planning to stay too, Huey?"

"Yeah."

"And how about you, Grace?"

"The research annex is like home to me. My family and I aren't close at all, so I don't have a compelling reason to leave."

Jade quickly turned to Mordred.

"And you, doc?"

"Oh, I'm going home. I can't wait to spend time with Emily without having to worry about anything."

"And Oscar?"

"Staying here with you all...would be rather difficult for me. There's much to prepare for the New Year's ceremony."

"Ah, okay!" Jade leaned back in his chair again. "As much as I'd like to stay, too, I'm needed back home. This may be our last get-together before the next term."

He sounded rather dispirited, but soon a look of determination appeared on his face. He stood up and pressed his fist to his chest.

"In which case, we've got to have enough fun today to make up for the long time when we won't see each other!"

And with that proclamation, their tea party officially got underway.

One hour later...

"So much for my tea party..."

Cecilia swept her gaze across the lounge, mortified. Jade was fast asleep, sprawled on top of a table. Eins had gotten weepy, while Zwei kept laughing for no reason. Mordred had passed out on a sofa in the corner. Huey was just staring vacantly, totally out of it. Oscar was sitting with his head in his hands, as if suffering from a head-ache. Dante, next to Oscar, was the only one seemingly unaffected, and he was enjoying himself as always.

This sorry state of affairs was the consequence of Dante's contribution to the party.

"Why did you have to bring booze?!" Gilbert yelled at him.

In Dante's glass was a beverage with a sweet fruity scent. He pouted.

"What, you're blaming me for this?"

"Who else do you think is to blame?!"

"I didn't force anyone to drink it. They helped themselves. Besides, this isn't booze. It's a juice made from drunken-berries!"

"Drunken-berries?" Cecilia had never heard of them.

Dante made a circle with his thumb and index finger and peeped at Cecilia through it.

"They're forest berries about this big. You press them, then boil them, and the liquid you get that way can make you woozy like alcohol."

"Really?"

"Yeah. And since it doesn't contain any alcohol, you don't pay the excise tax on it. Taverns used to sell it on the sly for cheap. I learned how to make it shortly after joining the organization."

So he made the beverage himself. Here was a man of many talents, ranging from assassination to juice-making.

"Still, it's misleading to pass it around saying it's just juice," groaned Gilbert, pressing his throbbing temples with his fingers.

Jade had been the first to start drinking. He took Dante's assurance that the drink was juice at face value and was eager to try it. Eins and Zwei followed suit. After sharing the equivalent of two, maybe three glasses, they were done for.

Grace and Gilbert had been wary of the beverage from the start and hadn't partaken. Neither did Lean and Cecilia, who'd gone to the restroom when Dante opened the bottle. Everyone else tried the drink and paid the price.

"I didn't lie, though! And what goes best with smoked meats? Alcohol, right? You should commend me for not bringing real booze." Dante puffed out his cheeks, surveying the casualties of his berry juice strewn around the room. "And Mordred was an accident. He mistook my glass for his."

"Poor Mordred. He didn't suspect that a student would bring liquor to a tea party."

"For the last time, it's NOT alcohol! Anyway, don't blame me for Oscar and Huey either. They knew what it was and drank it willingly!"

Dante pouted.

"They couldn't have known how potent it was. You've been gulping it down with no ill effect!"

"What can I say, I can hold my liquor."

"How about owning up?!" snapped Gilbert.

His angry attitude failed to wipe the smirk off Dante's face.

"Now, now, Gil, why are you getting so upset? Take a load off and have a glass. It tastes really good!"

"Cut it out already!"

"Ha-ha-ha!"

Not only was Dante unapologetic, but he was also having a great time riling up Gilbert. His victim found it like talking to a wall.

Cecilia and Lean just watched in silence. Cecilia was devastated; she'd gotten so excited for a fun tea party with her friends, and it ended before it even began. Plus, they'd barely touched the food.

"I'm so sorry about Huey, Lean…" Cecilia felt terrible for her friend.

"Hmm, Huey's kind of cute like this. Maybe I should have him drink more sometime…," Lean mused, lost in her thoughts. "Oh, did you say something?"

"Uh, no, nothing," Cecilia said quickly, not wanting to hear anything more about what Lean had planned for her boyfriend.

"G-Gil! Cec…il!" Jade groaned. He'd raised his head off the

table, but he was still very wobbly. His face was flushed red, and his eyes were shut. "My head…is spinning…"

"You've got to stop being so trusting, Jade."

"Ungh…"

"Can you stand?"

Gilbert sighed and wrapped Jade's arm around his shoulders to help him to his feet.

"Let's get you back to your room."

Jade was in no state to walk, so Gilbert practically had to carry him. Cecilia noticed he was having trouble, so she went around to take Jade's other arm. Before they left the lounge, Gilbert looked back.

"Oscar, we'll be back for you soon—"

"No need. I'll manage on my own. Just take care of Jade."

"All righty, and I'll take Huey back to his room!" Dante finished the rest of his drink and stood up.

That was it, then. They'd have to come back to help Mordred, Eins, and Zwei get to their rooms, one by one.

"We're not allowed in the boys' dorm anyway, so why don't we tidy up the lounge instead?" suggested Lean.

"Very well. Let's do that," agreed Grace.

The party had been far from a success.

"Our job's done, at last."

"Thank goodness!"

The sun was already low on the horizon when they dropped off Eins, the last of their juice-addled friends. Their get-together had started shortly after classes ended, but they wound up spending more time dragging everyone back to their rooms than having a good time.

Gilbert and Cecilia headed back to the lounge. They were already exhausted, but there was still tidying up left to do. Grace and Lean got started on that earlier, but there was so much mess, they probably hadn't finished with it yet.

"Things didn't turn out the way I had planned, but it wasn't all bad! We did spend some nice time together before that juice incident. And Becky's scones were a hit with everyone!"

"They sure were."

"Even you had a great time today."

"Huh? Did I?" Gilbert opened his eyes wide as if that were news to him.

Cecilia smiled.

"Uh-huh! I could tell! Especially toward the end of the party!"

"You don't mean…after everyone got hammered?"

"That's exactly what I mean!"

Gilbert gave her a look as if doubting her sanity. She ignored that and carried on.

"You're such good friends with everyone now."

"What makes you say that?"

"For one, you no longer get mad when they call you 'Gil.' And I know you'd never voluntarily help out someone you disliked."

Cecilia put her hands on her lower back and stretched backward. Then she turned to look at Gilbert, who was walking half a pace behind her.

"I was happy to see you enjoying yourself. It made it more fun for me, too!"

Gilbert came to a halt, thrown by both what she'd said and her big, uninhibited grin. But he only let his surprise show for a moment and quickly reassumed his earlier curmudgeonly expression. He hurried to catch up with her.

"You sure aren't an unapproachable loner now!"

"Are you referring to how I was in the game?"

"Huh? Ah, yeah! The way the original Cecilia treated you probably played a part in why you were so completely withdrawn…"

She dropped her gaze, feeling sorry for the in-game Gilbert. He was just a character in a game she'd played in her past life, but she empathized with him just the same as with the Gilbert standing in front of her now. He was the first character she'd romanced in the game, and the one she invested the most time in. Consequently, she'd developed quite an attachment to him.

"You were so lonely, and you barely came out of your room. I wanted you to have a better life this time around!"

"…"

"So seeing you tenderly taking care of the guys who got plastered today made me really emotional, you know? It made me feel so happy!"

Gilbert gazed at Cecilia in her wholesome cheer for a while. Then he made up his mind to say something he'd been sitting on for a while.

"Lean told me a few things about that game, too. So…was I your favorite?"

"H-huh?"

"Everyone's got a favorite character in that sort of game, right? Their game-crush."

Cecilia's face instantly turned bright red. She tripped up over her own feet when she realized that her blush was a dead giveaway.

"Er… Um…"

"I'm right, huh?"

Gilbert didn't sound overjoyed. He said it quite flatly, in fact. Cecilia went on the defensive.

"Y-you were my favorite, yes, but I wouldn't call that a crush! I wanted to protect you, to make you happy! It's…it's complicated!"

"Don't worry. I completely understand."

"You...you do?"

"Isn't that why you see me only as your little brother, no matter what I do?"

He sighed. Cecilia looked at him in confusion, not seeing how one thing related to the other.

"Don't worry about it. I was just thinking aloud," Gilbert said with a doleful smile.

Perhaps for the best, their conversation was about to be interrupted...

"That's where you were!"

"Grace! You were looking for us?" Cecilia called out to Grace who'd just came out from behind the corner.

Grace glanced at Gilbert, but it wasn't him she wanted to talk to. She walked over to Cecilia.

"Could we talk alone for a few minutes, Cecil?"

"Um, yeah. Sure," replied Cecilia, sensing urgency in her voice.

"What did you want to talk about?" Cecilia asked Grace once they went inside an empty classroom.

Grace lingered with her hand on the door she'd just closed while turned away from Cecilia, as if she was mulling something over. Then she turned slowly.

"I've been thinking a lot about this lately..."

"About what?"

"Prince Janis."

Cecilia straightened up, alert.

"Given what we know, we can be certain that the Dirk of Destiny is in his possession. On top of that, we do not have any means of tracking him down."

It was just as she'd said. They'd already exhausted all their options. Even the duke's connections hadn't helped them turn up any new leads. Marlin also mobilized her network of informers to search for Janis, but thus far she hadn't reported any findings. Cecilia had been pinning her hopes on Janis reaching out to her, but he hadn't tried to make contact in all this time, so her optimism was running out.

"You need to face the facts. It's impossible for us to track down Prince Janis."

"Let's not give up just yet—"

"You're betting on him contacting you, aren't you? But he has no reason to. Or to be precise, he has no reason to *want* to see Cecil again."

"Okay, so... Who else could lure him out?"

"Lean, possibly. As an assassination target, since she's a Holy Maiden candidate."

"A-assassination?!"

"She has Huey to protect her, though. Which may be enough of a deterrent to Prince Janis. He'd be unlikely to succeed at harming her even if he tried something."

That put Cecilia somewhat at ease. It did get her thinking, though. Since Janis' objective was to ruin the Kingdom of Prosper, he would certainly interfere with the Selection Ceremony. By targeting Lean.

"But let's stay on topic. What I wanted to tell you is that your plan for banishing the Obstructions has become unworkable."

Strangely, hearing that out loud didn't shock Cecilia. Deep down, she must have been thinking the same. She stared down at her feet, despondent. After an unnatural pause for a breath, Grace continued:

"If you still don't want to give up, there's something else you could try."

"I'll do anything!"

"If you can't find Janis, you'll have to force him to come out of hiding. He's a prince, not an outlaw. He wouldn't ignore official summons."

"You don't mean…"

Cecilia was gripped by anxiety. There were very few people in the world with the authority to summon a prince and actually have him show up.

"You will need Oscar's cooperation for this. Tell him the truth. There's no other way that I can think of."

Three days had passed since then. Cecilia was in the forest just outside of Algram. To her left was a river, swelling high against the bank after recent rains. To her right were steep crags. The road she was taking was wide enough for a horse-drawn carriage, but it wasn't paved, so puddles had formed here and there.

"I'm really sorry for troubling you with this…," apologized Elza.

She was standing in front of a group of six: Cecilia, Lean, Huey, Jade, Oscar, and Dante. Cecilia shook her head.

"It's no problem at all. Besides, we offered to help!"

"Still…I would normally be obliged to refuse assistance from outsiders, but it's a matter of urgency…" Elza dropped her gaze to the ground.

The matter in question was a problem the abbess had discovered last night. She'd arrived in the city with several of the nuns to make preparations for the Naissance Market. The market spanned almost a whole month, so they would need enough inventory to last at least a few days until they could get a new delivery in. The shrine was supposed to have sent them the goods that day, but they'd waited and waited in vain. Now they didn't have any merchandise to sell at their stall.

The nuns grew worried that something had happened to the transport, and eventually, a messenger came to tell them that the wagon had gotten stuck in a ditch. Worse still, it was badly damaged, so even if they got it back onto the road again, it wouldn't make a difference.

"At least the wagon got stuck near Algram. Our first thought was to go and pick up the parcels by ourselves…"

Except that the sisters couldn't get to it with another wagon because it would get mired in mud as well. They would have to carry the parcels out of the forest with their muscles alone, which was a tall order for a bunch of women who weren't used to strenuous physical activity. There were only five of them all together, so there was no way they could carry all the parcels out of the forest in one trip. Some might even be too heavy for them to lift. The wagon driver had to stay with his broken wagon until help arrived, so they couldn't count on him.

Fortunately, the academic term was over, and Cecilia and her friends happened to be visiting the Cigogne Orphanage, where Elza and the nuns were also staying. Huey was helping with the market preparations, Jade and Lean were discussing the publication of her next novel, Oscar was having a look around, and Dante was following him around. When they'd heard about Elza's problem, they offered to help right away, and so here they were now.

"Lots of forest routes are untraversable by wagon right now due to the heavy rains," remarked Jade, staring at the dark clouds shrouding the sky. It looked as if it might start raining again any moment.

Elza bowed her head low again.

"Your Highness, you honor me too much by assisting me with

this mundane task. You even went so far as to bring soldiers for the heavy lifting…"

"Don't mention it. And the troops will benefit from some exercise," Oscar replied in a stiff, formal tone.

Elza bowed her head again.

The soldiers and the nuns were walking a little way ahead of the rest of the group. Cecilia watched them absentmindedly, thinking about what Grace had told her three days earlier.

"You will need Oscar's cooperation for this. Tell him the truth. There's no other way that I can think of."

"Easy for her to say…," Cecilia muttered under her breath.

Lean had pointed out earlier that Oscar didn't pose a threat to her anymore, and she agreed. She could safely come out to him about her true identity. It might hurt his feelings, it might make him hate her, but he wouldn't try to harm her. At least so she believed.

But telling him now, after all that's happened…

How would Oscar take it when he learned that someone he'd become close friends with, who he thought was a guy, was in fact his fiancée? After dropping that bombshell, she couldn't straight up ask him for a huge favor like, "I'm also a Holy Maiden candidate! And I'm in big trouble! So please, please, please help me!"

I'd feel used if someone did that to me.

Being loyal and generous, Oscar would not turn down a request for help from a friend, no matter what, but Cecilia didn't want to trample over his feelings for the sake of her own interests.

She sighed, trudging onward with her head down. She was trying to imagine different scenarios in which she opened up to Oscar, but none of them were good.

Lean noticed that something was bugging her friend.

"What's the matter? Are you unwell?"

"I'm fine. Just stressing out about something Grace told me."

"Did it have to do with the Dirk of Destiny? Has she found anything?"

"No, nothing. It feels more like the progress we thought we'd made is lost…"

Cecilia wasn't sure what to tell her friend. Grace had shown her a way forward, but it was mentally taxing for Cecilia to even consider it.

Lean narrowed her eyes, unsatisfied by Cecilia's vague response.

"Not making progress doesn't mean we've lost anything, surely? Oh, on another note, I heard an interesting story from the nuns!"

"Tell me, tell me."

"They say a ghost of a nun has been haunting the shrine since a few months back! Lots of sisters have seen it!"

Cecilia looked at Lean sideways. Every old building came with a ghost story. There was even one about the old annex at their academy.

"Doesn't sound that strange to me."

"But here's the thing! This ghost stopped appearing after the night when we went looking for the dirk!"

"Huh…" Cecilia gave a response to show she was still listening, but she had no idea where her friend was going with this.

Lean crossed her arms and lowered her voice even more to make sure nobody but Cecilia could hear her.

"Which got me thinking that this ghost might have been Prince Janis!"

"Say what?!"

"He might have been searching for the dirk by night, wearing a nun's habit as a disguise!"

Lean put her index finger on Cecilia's nose and gave a smug grin, like a clever detective who'd just solved a case. Cecilia froze for a few seconds as she processed the plot twist. Then she pushed Lean's finger off her nose.

"You're reaching."

"Why?"

"Sure, Janis has a pretty face, but you can't mistake him for a woman. He's got wide shoulders, and he's so tall. There's no way he'd fool the nuns!"

"What about his bodyguard then? I haven't seen him, but maybe he could've pulled it off?"

"No, he's also well-built. Not that different from Janis."

"Oh, well…"

Lean retracted her hand, looking slightly disappointed.

"I also don't think that an outsider could get into the shrine so easily. We had to undergo checks even though we had an official letter of invitation. I don't see how someone could come and go every night without being detected."

The intruder would have to break in somehow, but the security at the shrine where the Holy Maiden lived was tight.

Lean put her hands on her hips, annoyed.

"But Janis did get in somehow! How did he do it then? Did he disguise himself as someone from the shrine?"

"Why are you asking me…?"

It was a mystery. The same went for how he'd learned of the Dirk of Destiny, hidden in the depths of the shrine—something only people who transmigrated from Cecilia's previous world could have knowledge of.

"What if—"

"Watch out, Cecil!" Jade yelled before Cecilia could finish her sentence.

She looked up and saw a huge boulder rolling down the cliffside. She moved away on instinct and managed to dodge it. The rock barreled past her thunderously and landed in the river. Lots of small stones followed.

"Holy…! The ground's unstable from all the rain!"

"Watch out, everyone! More rocks coming down!"

Cecilia activated her Artifact to protect her friends. It created an invisible dome around them. Small rocks shattered on contact with it, while large ones bounced off. But the dome didn't extend very far…

"Aah!"

"Elza!"

The abbess, who'd been walking ahead of them, was outside the protective dome. She crouched down in fear, covering her head. A mass of rocks was rolling down toward her.

"You hold this!"

Cecilia pressed her Artifact into Lean's hand. Her friend protested, but Cecilia paid her no attention. She jumped out of the dome and sprinted to where Elza was cowering on the ground.

"Are you okay?"

"Y-yes…"

Cecilia took her hand. The cleric was shaking, scared out of her wits.

"You'll be safe over there! Come on!"

But just as she tried to get Elza to stand up, the ground slid out from underneath her.

"Cecil! Elza!" Lean screamed.

Cecilia realized it was a landslide this time. The whole mass of earth they were standing on began to slide down toward the river.

"Nooo!"

"Uh…"

Cecilia grabbed Elza's arm, pulled her up to her feet, and pushed her into the dome. Dante caught her in his arms. Then Cecilia shouted over the roar of the landslide.

"Keep 'em safe, Lean!"

"What? No, you come—"

Cecilia didn't hear the rest. She blacked out.

It happened so fast that Oscar didn't even have the time to contemplate his powerlessness. When he saw his fiancée being carried away by the landslide, he leaped into action before any thought could form in his head, before any emotion had the chance to color his perception of the situation.

"You're in charge now, Dante!"

"Not so fast, Oscar!"

"Don't you dare try to stop me!"

Dante attempted to grab the prince, but Oscar shoved his hand away. But someone ought to have stopped him from attempting anything so foolish, or rather, he should have known better and stayed put. His body and mind weren't his alone. The prince belonged to the nation. He'd been born to become one of the cogs in the grand machine keeping it running. He wasn't allowed to put himself in harm's way. He wasn't allowed to let emotions get the better of him. All of his actions were to be guided by reason, cool rationality, for it was in the nation's best interest. Oscar was aware of this, of course. Painfully so.

The most logical course of action would have been to stay safe inside the protective dome and wait out the landslide before going out to search for Cecilia.

But that didn't feel like a choice he could make. It wasn't an option at all. Without her Artifact, her chances of survival were slim.

Oscar broke into a run and jumped into the river after Cecilia.

When Cecilia awoke, she found herself staring at an unfamiliar ceiling. This was the third time in the span of a year that this had happened. But on this occasion, she had come to in neither a carriage nor a cabin in the mountains. The ceiling appeared to be made of rock. Yet another new experience for her.

She sat up, her body leaden. A thin blanket slid down to her thighs. She looked around, her eyes not yet quite focused. She appeared to be inside a cave. Someone had lit a fire. Her wet outer clothes were spread out on a large rock next to another set of clothing, in a size bigger than hers, on a large rock to dry.

Wooden boxes were lined up by the walls. Perhaps this cave was a stopping place for hunters. The blanket she'd been covered with must have come from one of those boxes.

"But who put it over me...? Argh!"

Cecilia doubled over in pain. She was hurting all over. She rolled up the sleeves of her undershirt and found that she was bruised blue. The current of the river had battered her against rocks. Anywhere her skin had been exposed, like her hands and ankles, was covered in scrapes. There was a stinging pain in her cheeks and neck, so her face probably wasn't in good shape either. On the back of her hand were deep gashes, still bleeding. She opened and closed her hands a few times.

It sure hurts, but at least I can move...

"I survived?"

"Were you not expecting to?"

"Huh?"

She looked up and saw someone standing by the entrance to the cave. He had red hair and was naked from the waist up. She couldn't make out his face in the dark, though.

"Eek!" she squealed as he started to approach.

"Come, now. It's just me."

"Oh... I didn't recognize you for a moment there, Oscar..."

"I thought you weren't going to wake up."

She heard deep relief in his voice. He must have been worried sick. He crouched next to her and wiped something off her cheek and forehead. She guessed it was dirt. The warmth of his touch was comforting. She smiled, reassured that everything would be okay now that she'd made it.

"Are you hurt badly?"

"It kind of stings all over..."

"I'm sorry."

Oscar gazed at her with sympathy, but he seemed relieved that she was in good enough shape to talk without issue. He stood up and sat down across from her. For a while, the only sound in the cave was the crackling of the bonfire in front of them. Then Oscar spoke.

"I had a look outside. I'm not familiar with these parts, but it doesn't look like the river carried us very far. I made markers, so that the others should find us easily once they start checking down the river."

"Why don't we just walk back?"

"Not a good idea. It's a long uphill trek to the road. We wouldn't make it until morning, and it's not safe to wander around a surging river at night anyway."

Cecilia turned her head toward the entrance of the cave. It wasn't yet pitch-black outside, but the sky was already a dark blue. Oscar was right; they'd better give up on hiking back to the road.

"Ah, right." She turned back toward him. "Kind of late to be saying this, but I think I owe you for saving my life?"

"You don't owe me anything, but I did save you."

"I don't know how to thank you enough!"

"It's fine…"

Wait, what's up with him?

There was something off about Oscar. He didn't seem hurt, but he kept avoiding her gaze. Worried, Cecilia prodded his arm with one finger.

"Oscar?"

"Ceci…"

She got him to look at her, but he froze up for a moment before shutting his eyes and rubbing his forehead.

Is he…angry at me?

Why hadn't she thought of that before? She had acted so recklessly. She'd only been thinking about saving Elza, without realizing that she would need to protect herself, too. Oscar risked his life to pull her out of that river. He had a good reason to be upset.

Cecilia hung her head and apologized sincerely.

"I'm sorry, Oscar, I'm such an idiot! You could've died because of me! I'm really, really sorry!"

"You certainly are an impulsive one, but promise me this…"

"Y-yeah?"

"Don't run off to another country. Please."

"Wait, what?"

Having no clue what this was about, she gave him a puzzled look.

"Haven't you noticed anything?" he asked, a little exasperated.

She still didn't know what he was getting at, but rather than ask for clarification, she tried to figure it out on her own.

We're in a cave...sitting in front of a campfire, with our clothes drying next to it. The blanket Oscar put on me is covering my lap...

"Huh?"

Something didn't feel right when she looked down at the blanket, but she couldn't quite out her finger on it. She was wearing a shirt and pants. The blanket was over her lap, with her wounded hands resting on top of it.

Cecilia kept glancing from her shirt to her pants, to the blanket, to the wounds on her hands, and back again.

It's...the shirt?

She finally realized what was wrong. Her top. It felt too tight; the third button down her neck was threatening to come undone, exposing her naked skin underneath.

It's a men's shirt, so of course it's too tight there... Huh? Wait a second...

She brought a hand to her chest. It was plump to the touch.

"Oh no!"

Panicking, she pulled the blanket up to her chin. Her body felt hot, and it wasn't only because of the blanket. She furtively glanced down under it. There was no doubt about it—the sash she'd used to bind her breasts had come undone. It must have happened when she'd fallen into the river.

Cecilia pulled her knees to her chest, trying to make herself look smaller. Something tickled her shoulder. She reached around to see if a string or something had gotten stuck to her clothing.

That's no string! It's my hair! Have I lost my wig, too?!

Her honey-blond hair was loosely draped over her back.

She'd been sitting there next to Oscar without her wig, with her breasts conspicuously struggling against the shirt she was wearing.

"I... Er..." Her voice was shaking.

She glanced at Oscar and saw that he was also glancing at her out of the corner of his eye.

"It—it's been a long time since we last met, Your Highness…"

"Are you seriously going to pretend I pulled Cecilia out of the river by chance after diving in to save Cecil? That you're different people?"

She wasn't sure why she'd even thought to give that a try. Oscar wasn't stupid.

"Uh… Um…"

"Could you just talk to me normally? It's getting late, we're both tired, and you're making things awkward."

"I will… I'll try…"

She dropped the formality but didn't know what to say to him. Instead, she gazed at the bonfire, her thoughts racing.

The plan was to eventually tell him that she'd been attending the academy in disguise, but she hadn't wanted the big reveal to happen out of her control. All the lines she'd been rehearsing were useless now.

Oscar tried to break the ice.

"May I call you Cecilia now? If you'd rather I still called you Cecil, that's also fine by me…"

"Um… Cecilia's fine…"

"Okay."

"…"

"…"

The tense silence continued.

It's stressing me out so much!

She was the one making things difficult, really, but the awkwardness was just as unbearable for her as it was for Oscar.

125

If it only was a normal day on campus, she'd be able to flee from the situation. The loaded atmosphere was giving her severe anxiety. But she was in a cave in the middle of a forest, it was the middle of the night, and it had just started raining. There was nowhere else for her to go. She was stuck there with Oscar.

What do I do now...?

Pale and distressed, Cecilia curled up and stared at the ground. Oscar picked up a dry log and threw it into the bonfire. The fire crackled louder and flames briefly rose up higher.

Cecilia stole a glance at Oscar's profile. His expression was neutral as usual, maybe slightly expectant. But he wasn't angry or annoyed with her.

"Can I ask you something, Oscar?"

"Sure."

"Maybe I'm bad at reading you, but you don't seem all that surprised?"

"I'm not."

"Don't tell me you knew it was me for some time?"

He looked at her like he couldn't quite believe she'd said that. After blinking a few times, he turned back to the fire.

"I did," he admitted, after a hesitant pause.

"Since when?"

"Last summer."

"What?!" her voice came out in a falsetto.

Cecilia had thought it might have been a few days, or maybe weeks, since he'd seen through her disguise. Never would she have suspected that he'd been onto her for almost half a year. And if he'd noticed it was her last summer, then it must have been during the field trip...

"Was...was it when we were sharing a cottage?"

"Yeah."

"Why didn't you say anything?!" she exclaimed accusingly without thinking.

Oscar wasn't bothered by her suddenly belligerent attitude.

"Because Gilbert told me you'd flee the country if you knew that I knew."

"What?"

"You wouldn't do that?"

"No… I mean, maybe…"

If she'd known then that her disguise had failed her, she might have considered that, actually. Back when she'd been terrified he might kill her.

So that's why he told me not to run away earlier…

That also shed a new light on a lot of past events. Ever since that summer in the Sylvie cottage, Oscar had been hanging out with and helping Cecil knowing he was really Cecilia.

Ugh, my head hurts!

She thought back to all the things she'd said to him or about him, and about how she'd treated him; it made her so embarrassed she wanted to crawl in a hole. And now he'd even saved her life!

Oscar could see that she was agonizing over something, although he couldn't have guessed what was going on in her head.

"Anyway… Are you warm enough?"

"Y-yeah, the fire's keeping me toasty. Sorry I'm hogging the blanket."

"Don't worry about it. My clothes should be dry soon… You're still doing your Cecil voice. It's a little weird."

"Well, you told me to talk to you like I used to!"

"Yes, but not like that!"

Oscar chuckled. Cecilia smiled briefly, but her expression soon turned serious again.

"Oscar, I…I'm really sorry."

"Hmm?"

"About not telling you it was me. I can only imagine how awful it must have made you feel…"

He wasn't showing much emotion, but he could have been angry or hurt. She wouldn't blame him if he decided to cut all ties with her after this.

Cecilia clenched her fists, steeling herself for what he might say in response.

"I thought you were too much of airhead to realize that."

"Now that's mean! I'm not that dumb!"

"I was only teasing," he said with a lighthearted chuckle. "It didn't make me feel awful. But I was sad about it."

"Why?"

"Because you didn't trust me. Gilbert knew the truth, of course, but so did Lean, and Dante. I didn't understand why I wasn't allowed into your trusted circle of friends, and it made me feel pitiful."

Cecilia had been expecting to hear words of disdain and rebuke, not sorrow. She opened her eyes wide.

"You wanted me to trust you?"

"Of course. I'm your fiancé."

"How can you spend your life together with someone if you don't have mutual trust? Or…did you forget about our engagement?"

"No, how could I forget?! What you're saying…makes a lot of sense, actually…"

Embarrassed, she hung her head. Cecilia's cheeks were burning, and her whole body felt warmer. For the first time, she had this intense realization that this was the man who she was to marry.

"Do you not want to wed me?" he asked slowly.

"Huh?"

"Is that the reason you were pretending to be a boy?"

"…"

"Is that why you didn't want me to discover your true identity?"

His voice was calm, but tinged with sadness and anxiousness. Cecilia jumped to her feet.

"N-no!"

"No?"

"I had a…a special reason not to tell you. But it's not that I didn't want to marry you!"

To be fair, she'd never given serious thought to their engagement. She'd assumed Oscar would fall in love with Lean, like in the game. A happy marriage between him and Cecilia wasn't in any of the game's scenarios. So she never thought it would really happen.

Oscar was silent for a while after hearing her emotional reply.

"Is that so?"

"Yes!"

"You're okay with marrying me?"

"Yes," she nodded, a bit surprised he was asking for confirmation so many times.

Oscar grinned mischievously.

"So I've got your word now."

"Huh?"

"Which makes it final. I won't be seeking to dissolve our engagement, I assure you."

"Wait, what?" her voice came out in a squeak.

Oscar looked up at Cecilia, who was still standing in front of him. His gaze was steady, firm with resolve.

"You said you're not against the marriage."

"I'm not, I guess."

"Then I won't let you go. You matter too much to me now."

He took her hand in his and gave her a squeeze. His palm was warmer than hers, and somehow that heat made her feel giddy.

"I promise to be a devoted husband," he said as if making his vows there and then.

Cecilia blushed.

"I think I've had too much for one day," she said, plopping back onto the cave floor, dizzy from the tidal wave of emotions.

It was vital for Oscar to understand this, but he was struggling to wrap his head around it.

"Could you repeat that last part again?"

"Come on, it's pretty straightforward! You were supposed to hate my guts so much you'd have me executed! And Lean and I would have been archenemies to begin with!"

Oscar rubbed his forehead, processing this unbelievable version of events Cecilia was presenting to him. Based on her memories from a past life… Not only was that fact incredible in itself, but Cecilia was retelling the story out of order, so it still wasn't making any sense no matter how many times he had her repeat it.

No, that wasn't quite true. He understood the gist of what she was saying—he was hearing the words. But he couldn't accept it. Or rather, he didn't want to.

How could I be destined to kill Cecilia?

He couldn't comprehend what this "game" she was referring to was, but it seemed to boil down to fact that Cecilia was born into this world knowing the future. It was hard to swallow that his future options would almost guarantee him becoming Cecilia's enemy. He couldn't even conceive of any event which might turn him against her.

But what confused him even more was…

"So anyhow, that's why I was pretending to be a guy!"

…Cecilia's conclusion. Oscar kept rubbing his forehead, trying to find the logic in what she was saying.

I just don't get it…

Gilbert had told him that he wouldn't understand Cecilia's motives for cross-dressing. At the time, Oscar had thought he was being taken for a fool, but it turned out that her brother was spot-on.

"And actually, it would be so great if you could help me get the Dirk of Destiny off Prince Janis…," Cecilia finished her long explanations with a request.

Oscar considered it carefully before giving her his reply.

"That, I can do. The Nativity ritual is coming up. I could summon Janis for the occasion—what do you think? I was going to send out invitations to Nortracha soon, anyway, so I could add his name to the list."

"But is that really okay? Won't it cause you or the king any trouble?"

"You can rely on me, Cecilia, I assure you." Oscar crossed his arms. "I'll come up with an excuse. The Dirk of Destiny rightfully belongs to Torche, but Prince Janis isn't known for obeying the law, so I cannot make him return the dagger through official channels."

"Yeah, figures…"

"But what are you going to do when you meet him? He's not the type you can negotiate with."

Cecilia puffed out her chest and patted it.

"Oh, I have a plan for that!"

"A plan you came up with all on your own? That doesn't inspire confidence."

"You're being mean again!"

"No. Realistic."

Cecilia didn't have the best track record when it came to clever schemes. They'd reliably turned out to be unreliable.

"Let's discuss it with Gilbert. I don't know yet how else I could be of assistance, but I'll do anything in my power for you."

"Super! Thanks, Oscar!"

Cecilia wasn't in disguise, but still had Cecil's energy.

She is Cecil.

It was reassuring. Cecilia wasn't like what he had imagined based on their childhood encounter, but that wasn't a bad thing. He actually loved her even more like this.

Not having noticed his thoughtful, tender gaze, Cecilia stood up, restless with energy. She clenched her hands into fists, as if she were raring to go confront Prince Janis right then and there.

"All right! Let's do this, Oscar!"

"It's great that you're psyched, but you need to take some time out to recover first."

"Right! My tummy took a nasty whacking. It hurts pretty bad."

In one swift move, she lifted up her shirt to show him. Oscar silently screamed.

"Cover yourself!"

"You're one to talk! You're not even wearing a shirt!"

She seemed perfectly okay with baring her belly in front of him. He hoped it wasn't because she'd gotten so used to her Cecil persona that she'd forgotten she wasn't just another guy.

Maybe Cecilia didn't realize that even just her stomach could have an effect on people.

Poor Gilbert...

Cecilia giggled, unaware that she'd quickened Oscar's pulse. He couldn't help but feel sympathy for his long-suffering rival. If he were in Gilbert's shoes, he might already have been driven to insanity.

Cecilia tucked her shirt back in and looked up at Oscar.

"By the way, where's your shirt? I don't see it drying on the rocks?"

"Hmm? Ah, I folded it up to use as a pillow for you. I'd forgotten about it."

"What?!"

She quickly spun around to look at where she'd been lying on the ground. Oscar had wanted to make her at least a little more comfortable on the hard rock floor. He thought about putting his coat down for her to lie on, but it was soaked, so it would have only made her colder.

"You needn't have bothered! We've got to get it dry, too!"

She snatched it off the ground. It was sopping wet. He'd wrung it out before folding it and putting it under her head, but her hair was drenched, too, and the shirt had soaked up all that moisture. It was as if they'd just fished it out of the river.

"I'm so sorry... You must be cold."

"I'll be fine once I put my coat back on," he assured her, not wanting her to feel bad about his small act of kindness.

Cecilia took the blanket off her shoulders and eagerly offered it to Oscar.

"Then you should at least have the blanket. Please, take it. I'm warm enough now."

"No, you keep it. Don't worry about me."

"No, but—"

"You're wearing a wet shirt, so you need it more than I do."

He could just take his shirt off to dry it, but he wouldn't have dared remove hers while she was asleep, so it had never gotten the chance to dry. And of course, wet clothes didn't keep you warm.

"Hmm, okay...," she admitted after a brief moment of hesitation.

Cecilia put the blanket over her shoulders again, but she spread it out wide. Oscar noticed how her shirt stuck to her skin, revealing all her curves.

"How about we share it?"

He shifted farther back and *bam*! Banged his head against the wall.

She can't be serious...

Oscar was beyond shocked, to the point he felt anger rise within him. He wasn't some old man who'd long lost his drive and could calmly share a blanket with his crush, sitting next to him in a wet top that had turned almost see-through and left very little to the imagination. No, he was a hormonal young man struggling to maintain control over his body.

He scooted farther away from her.

"I'm fine as I am, thank you!"

"But—"

"I said I'm fine! Don't come any closer!"

He never would have thought he'd utter those words to her. Cecilia was trying to sidle up to him, still offering the edge of the blanket, innocent and well-meaning.

"Come on, you must be chilly."

"On the contrary! I'm burning up at the moment!"

"Don't be so shy."

"I wish you were a little more shy right now!"

Thoughtlessly, he stood up and walked away from her, until his back was pressed against the cold wall of the cave. He was half naked, but his body was burning. Cecilia found his behavior alarming and followed after him, concerned. She really had no survival instinct. Stopping in front of him, she peered with worry into his eyes.

"What's wrong, Oscar?"

"You..."

"Yes?"

"You matter too much to me!"

Just a few minutes earlier, he'd been promising to be a good husband to her one day. Oscar wanted to be respectful and take things slowly with her, but here Cecilia was, a slab of meat next to a starving wolf. Did she not comprehend that other kind of hunger? Then how could he explain? His craving was real and urgent, and it was only through an extraordinary feat of self-restraint that he was able to keep his bestial instincts at bay.

"I don't understand. What are you doing?"

"I should be asking you the same question! What on earth are you up to?!"

"Um… I'm just trying to share the blanket with you?"

"You can't be serious!"

"It's okay. Come on, let's share it."

Oscar felt as if the walls of the cave were closing in on him.

"You'll catch a cold if you stay like this…" she said to him as if he were a stubborn child.

He couldn't care less if he got sick.

"Come closer…"

"NO!"

He tried to push her arm away when she tried to cover him with the blanket…

"Whoa!"

But he miscalculated and accidentally shoved her back. Cecilia lost her balance and would've crashed hard onto the rock floor had Oscar not grabbed her, putting his other hand on the back of her head to pull her back up…except that his knees buckled under him after doing this, and he fell forward. His palms throbbed. His knees were pure pain. The hand he'd placed on the back of Cecilia's head had smashed against the floor.

"S-sorry…"

"Huh?"

Oscar opened his eyes and realized he'd fallen over on top of Cecilia.

"Argh!"

This was too much. He couldn't breathe. His lips were trembling, and his fingertips were ice cold. He couldn't take it anymore. He swore inwardly.

"Um, Oscar?"

Her voice, so close to him. His heart was beating so rapidly, he feared it might explode. Oscar gritted his teeth.

Wasn't it okay to let go now? Hadn't he proven himself to her, put up with so much for her already? He'd confessed his love to her, and she was okay with becoming his wife. If something happened now between them, it wouldn't really be a problem, would it?

Just as Oscar began giving in to the evil whispers in his head, he heard rustling outside the cave.

"You hear that?"

Cecilia tensed up in his embrace, alert.

"Shh. I've got this."

Oscar's sanity returned at once. He made sure not to make any noise as he listened keenly for any more sounds from the outside...

"Cecil? Your Highness? Are you in there?" And after a short pause, "Well, now..."

"Huh?"

"It's Gil!" Cecilia exclaimed with happy relief.

She was still pinned down by Oscar, who'd gone pale. Gilbert wore a stony expression. Oblivious to the mood in the cave, Cecilia wriggled out from under Oscar and trotted over to her brother, overjoyed to see him.

"You found us, Gil! Yay! My disguise got ruined when I fell into the river and—"

"You don't need to say anything."

Gilbert put his coat over Cecilia and started leading her out, completely ignoring Oscar, who was still on all fours on the floor.

"Gilbert! It's not what you think! I didn't... We didn't...," the prince called out.

"I'm not talking to you, you piece of garbage." He gave Oscar a look more terrifying than he'd ever seen.

It was the day after Gilbert had rescued Cecilia from Osca...from the cave, rather.

"Say, Gil... Are you angry...?"

"I'm amazed that you'd have doubts about that," Gilbert replied with a smile so chilling, Cecilia pulled her quilt up to her nose to hide behind it.

"I—I was just checking...," she replied in a trembling voice.

They were in Cecilia's room. She was running a fever, likely as a consequence of having fallen into that cold river the other day. Doctor Mordred had taken care of her injuries, but he couldn't do much about her illness and general exhaustion, so she was resting up in bed, free of her wig or any other parts of her disguise.

Gilbert was sitting on a stool next to her bed, cutting an apple for her. He was shaping the peel on each slice into rabbit ears. Apple bunnies always made Cecilia happy.

He addressed her without looking up from his work.

"You need to stop being so careless, Cecilia."

"Yes, I know…"

She looked very contrite, as if she had learned her lesson after both the incident with Janis and the landslide, but Gilbert was certain this lesson would be forgotten in an instant once she got some other crazy idea in her head again. It was just the way she was. He stole a glance at her and sighed.

Well, this time it wasn't so much her fault, though…

To be fair, Cecilia had tried being more cautious by taking Dante along with her for Janis' stakeout, and Elza might not have made it without Cecilia risking her life to rescue her. But from Gilbert's point of view, it was all very much unnecessary. Cecilia should've stopped Eins and Zwei from going to see Janis that day, by force if necessary. And in his eyes, Elza's life was worth far less than Cecilia's, so it if anyone was going to have a brush with death, he'd sacrifice the cleric.

Yet Cecilia wasn't the type to abandon a friend in need, no matter the danger it put her in. And since her kindness was one of the traits which had made him fall in love with her, he'd have to put up with her not putting her best interests before everything else.

Gilbert changed the subject as he moved a piece of apple around in his hand, deftly carving out little rabbit ears.

"Moving on… Did Oscar really not do anything to you?"

"He didn't! You saw!"

"I'm asking precisely because of what I saw when I walked into that cave."

His voice practically became a growl at the memory. That night, he'd been running through the forest, desperately searching for Cecilia, fearing the worst. When he saw Oscar's cravat tied around a branch as a sign for the search party, he felt almost weak with relief... Then he entered the cave near the marked tree and saw a sight he'd been entirely unprepared for.

Oscar lying on top of Cecilia.

A cold void manifested in Gilbert's heart, consuming any warmth that had been within him. He normally treated his rival with gentlemanly politeness, but he hadn't been able to address the man with anything other than pure contempt at that moment.

"I don't think you're as angry as you make it out to be."

"What makes you think so?"

"I dunno... Just a gut feeling?"

Most of what Cecilia said and did in life was based on her gut. Gilbert reluctantly nodded.

"There are alleviating circumstances. Oscar did save your life, after all."

And despite what he'd said, Gilbert didn't actually think Oscar was trying to have his way with Cecilia back there in the cave. Knowing how clumsy and thoughtless Cecilia could be, his bet was on her having done something dumb, and Oscar falling over on top of her in an attempt to help. The prince was straight as an arrow, and a bit dense, too, so Gilbert could see how things could've turned out that way.

"You should tell Oscar that you're not really mad at him."

"Why?"

"Because he was freaking out!" she said with a laugh.

Oscar had followed after them all the way from the cave to the carriage trying to speak to Gilbert, begging him to listen and swearing that he hadn't done anything. Gilbert had been too incensed to even acknowledge him.

In retrospect, I was being immature too..., Gilbert thought.

"He really wants to be friends with you."

"Sorry, what?"

"That's why he asked you to use his name and not title him 'His Highness', no?"

"But why are you bringing this up now?"

Oscar had asked him to drop the formality years ago, but Gilbert insisted on treating him with reserve. Gilbert frowned, wondering why Cecilia was reminding him of that.

"Because it's time you admitted that you two are actually friends? You're always coming up with fake reasons not to like him, but if that was how you really felt, you wouldn't have the urge to explain why. I'm aware that you don't bother with people at all when they don't matter to you."

She gave him a "know-it-all" face. Gilbert sighed.

"Maybe I'll consider it."

He showed Cecilia the finished apple slices.

"Yay! Bunnies!"

"You sound like a child, getting excited about your rabbit apples. Here."

"Yum! Yum! Thanks!"

"Hmm..."

She seemed almost giddy—it must have been the fever. Gilbert pressed the back of his hand to her forehead, then traced it down to her cheek.

"Your fever's not going down yet. You should try to sleep when you finish the apple."

"Okay!"

Gilbert smiled with his eyes at her, glad she was following his advice for a change.

It took only ten minutes for Cecilia to fall asleep. She had a second slice of apple and a few sips of water before her eyelids suddenly closed, and she drifted off in the middle of a conversation. The ordeal from the day before had taken a toll on her body.

Gilbert stroked her cheek one more time, needing to touch her to make sure that she really was there, that he hadn't lost her in that river.

"Thank goodness you're safe…," he whispered, speaking from his heart.

When someone told him that Cecilia had been carried away by the river, he'd felt as if the world had ended for a moment. She'd always been careless, but death seemed to positively stalk her since she enrolled in the academy. Gilbert wanted to kick himself for not fully believing her about the game, her past life, and her being fated to die.

Cecilia stirred in her sleep, sensing his touch. Gilbert smiled upon seeing her so peaceful, then quietly left the room.

To his surprise, someone was waiting just outside.

"And what are you doing here, Your Highness?"

"I came to check on Cecilia, but I heard your voice…"

Oscar scratched his cheek awkwardly. He'd been standing outside the room to avoid interrupting them.

Gilbert softly closed the door behind him.

"You're out of luck. She's sleeping now," he said to Oscar in an unfriendly tone.

"I'll have to come back some other time then," said the prince, handing a small box to Gilbert.

It was from a famous Algram chocolatier. It had a faint sweet scent of cocoa.

"Why are you giving me this?"

"It's for Cecilia. Could you give it to her?"

"Why don't you give it to her yourself?"

"You're saying that now, but you'd get mad at me if I went into her room with no one else around."

"Of course I would."

"Well, then I can't give it to her myself, can I?!" Oscar shouted, exasperated by Gilbert's self-contradictory advice.

Not only did Gilbert not flinch at Oscar's exclamation, but his demeanor grew even chillier.

"Why do you even care what I say?"

"Sorry?"

"You're her fiancé. It shouldn't matter to you if it bothers me that you'd be in the room alone with her. You know she's not going to run away just because you've discovered her secret, either. So why don't you just do whatever you please, regardless of whether I like it or not?" Gilbert practically spat the words at him. What he was saying wasn't rude, but his embittered attitude made it come across as such.

He'd anticipated that this would happen one day—that he'd lose his advantage over Oscar, if you could call it that, when the prince learned the truth about Cecil. That the fact he'd been close to Cecilia for over a decade might not amount to much after that.

Oscar was a prince, and Cecilia's fiancé. If he were in Oscar's place, Gilbert wouldn't give a damn about her adoptive brother's objections.

That said, Prince Oscar had been listening quietly. He sighed and looked at the ground after Gilbert said his piece.

"It wouldn't sit right with me to use my position to get what I want. And while I have no intention to annul my engagement to Cecilia, I don't consider myself to have any special privileges when it comes to her, unless she grants me them herself. We've been interacting as friends for so long. Don't you think it might make her uncomfortable if I acted overly familiar all of a sudden?"

"Possibly."

"Plus, I wouldn't want to antagonize a friend."

"What friend?" Gilbert looked at Oscar. "You mean, her as Cecil?"

"No. You."

"What?!" Gilbert's voice cracked.

Oscar frowned.

"Aren't we friends? You offered me your friendship first, didn't you?"

"Did I say something along those lines? That was just..."

Something he'd uttered out of politeness, without meaning much by it, at the start of the academic year. Back when Oscar had still been badgering Gilbert to let him see Cecilia.

Gilbert's response visibly crushed Oscar.

"I hadn't realized... Oh, well."

Gilbert's lips curved even farther down and his eyelids dropped halfway.

"Urgh. Enough of this already..."

Gilbert sighed, feeling deflated. This was becoming ridiculous. It would be in his best interest to keep Oscar at a distance. Their personalities were incompatible. Not to mention that they were romantic rivals. Yet somehow Oscar had come to like him, and they'd been through so much together that even Gilbert was getting used to having him around. What clinched it, though, was the fact that Oscar was ready to die in order to save Cecilia. That selfless act bought him Gilbert's eternal gratitude.

Gilbert swept past Oscar and started walking down the hallway. The prince turned around, flustered.

"H-hey!"

"Let's go, Osc. There are plans to be made, and we're short on time," said Gilbert, looking back at him.

Oscar was so surprised to hear Gilbert use a nickname for him that he froze on the spot. Then he smiled wryly.

"We'd better get started, then."

He followed after Gilbert, quickening his pace until he caught up. They started walking together.

"Do you have any ideas yet?"

"A few. Little can be done unless we enlist the help of more people, which will be the first hurdle."

"I can take care of that."

"Excellent."

They went over what needed doing as matter-of-factly as usual. Eventually, however, Oscar blurted out what had been on his mind.

"That aloof coldness of yours is just an act, isn't it?"

"What are you talking about?"

Gilbert shot him a hateful look, but the loathing he tried to convey failed to come across quite as genuine as it used to.

✦ CHAPTER 4 ✦ Showdown

It was December 24, the night of the Nativity. The royal palace was very quiet, and a guard on night duty standing by the palace gate did a big yawn.

"Have you no shame? Be more serious about your job!" The guard standing on the other side of the gate scolded him.

The bored guard had tears in his eyes from that massive yawn. He pouted at his partner.

"I'm doing it just fine. Not like we're going to even see anyone until the shift ends. Except guests going out for a stroll, maybe."

"There are many important guests staying at the palace right now, though. We can't allow an incident to occur because of our inattention."

"Right, right!"

The lazy guard on the left side of the gate rolled his eyes at the serious guard on the right.

Every year, an evening party celebrating the Nativity was hosted at the palace. It wasn't a huge affair, but it was an opportunity for the local upper echelons of society to mingle with diplomats and eminent nobles from neighboring countries the Kingdom of Prosper had good relations with.

"Did you hear that they also invited the Nortracha royals this year?"

"Huh. That's new. They don't normally invite foreign royalty, right?"

"Apparently, it's because His Highness Oscar wishes to talk to Prince Janis about the future of our nations."

"Oof, imagine living with so much responsibility on your shoulders."

There was a sudden movement of air between the guards. Only the one on the left picked up on it and looked around.

"Something wrong?"

"Hmm, no. It was just the wind."

The guard on the right straightened his back.

"Don't get distracted by every little thing. We've got to be alert and keep intruders out. Imagine what punishment would await us if we let an uninvited guest get into the palace!"

"Don't want to even think of that."

The guard on the left finally straightened up and concentrated on staring intently ahead.

"Whew! That was nerve-racking!"

Three silhouettes appeared out of thin air. First Jade, then Eins and Zwei. Jade put away his Artifact, which he'd used to get the three of them inside the palace. Then he looked around to make sure they were in the clear.

"I think it's safe to say we made it."

"Phew! I was so nervous when I saw the guards!"

"Same, same! I had my heart in my mouth when we were passing right next to them!"

"Scaredy-cats," said Eins, looking at his shaking hands with disapproval.

The hallway they were in was a waiting area for special guests, so it didn't see much use. It was lit, but only dimly, and there was nobody around.

Jade still couldn't stop shaking.

"It's my first time gaining unauthorized entry into the palace, you know."

"I'm terrified someone might spot us."

"Yeah, we'd be in so much trouble!"

Jade and Zwei clasped each other's palms. Eins put a hand on his hip.

"Why did you put up your hands for this mission if you can't even keep your cool?"

"I wanted to help Cecil..."

"I thought I could do it, but I'm really overwhelmed now that I'm actually here..."

"You're like two peas in a pod, I swear," grumbled Eins.

He may have been Zwei's twin brother, but Jade had more in common with his sibling personality-wise.

The reason the three friends had secretly entered the palace came down to Cecil, of course. He'd told them about the Dirk of Destiny and Janis' abilities a week earlier. Soon after the landslide incident, from which he had thankfully escaped unharmed, Cecil summoned all of Lean's Knights, along with Gilbert and Huey, to make a request of them.

* * *

"I have to retrieve the Dirk of Destiny from Prince Janis, and I need your help."

Mordred explained the knife's properties, and Cecil confirmed that the item was without a doubt in the possession of Janis. A dagger that could eliminate Obstructions from the world—it sounded almost too good to be true. Everyone agreed to help.

"I wasn't expecting to be assigned a high-profile task like this!"

"Same! I thought I'd be on lookout duty or helping with some minor stuff."

"Getting hand-picked for the palace infiltration and dirk retrieval squad isn't something I saw coming either…"

Cecil's plan went as followed: First, Oscar would invite Janis for the Nativity on some excuse. Once he arrived at the palace, Jade would use his Artifact to secretly enter the grounds together with Eins and Zwei. They would then break into Janis' room to see if the dirk was there.

"After that, I'll use my Duplication ability to make a copy of it…"

"…and then I'll use Transfer to send the original to Lean."

The twins repeated the instructions, looking at each other.

Lean, Huey, and Mordred were already waiting near the White Shrine, having entered the grounds earlier with the help of Jade's Artifact. Upon receiving the Dirk of Destiny, Lean and her team would proceed to the innermost altar of the shrine. They chose not to wait inside the building to make sure the current Holy Maiden couldn't sense their presence.

"Hold on, if what Janis said is true, isn't everyone at the shrine our enemy? If they're the ones sowing the seeds of Obstructions." Zwei had a sudden thought.

"Maybe not. Cecil said they might not be aware of what they're doing, remember? You shouldn't assume they're against us without any evidence," Eins said decisively, hoping to dispel his anxious brother's worries.

"They made a very good impression on me, for what that's worth. It's wise to be cautious, but we shouldn't suspect them of the worst just because Janis wanted us to."

"Right… That makes me feel better," Zwei nodded to himself a few times, convinced by Eins and Jade.

Having been betrayed by someone he'd trusted in the past, Zwei still found it difficult to have confidence in people.

"I wonder if everything's going okay for Cecil's team, too…"

"I can't think of a stronger group than Cecil, Oscar, and Gilbert. They'll be fine," Jade asserted with absolute confidence.

They stopped in front of Janis' room.

"Those three have the toughest task, though—keeping Janis occupied until we're done here," Eins said with a worried sigh.

"Achoo!"

Cecilia sneezed in front of the door to the hall where that night's party was being held. She was accompanied by Gilbert in his finery.

"Are you still feeling unwell? That cold hasn't passed yet, has it?"

"Oh no, I'm totally fine! I just felt a little chilly. I'm not used to wearing this sort of outfit anymore!"

"Come to think of it, it's been forever since I last saw you like this."

"Ha-ha… I've been living the life of a recluse for a while, giving all social gatherings a miss," Cecilia said with a bashful smile.

She was wearing a dress. It was blue like a shimmering sea and adorned with sparkly jewels, with fine lace at the neckline and layered pleats from the hips down that resembled waves. This gorgeous dress accentuated her slender porcelain-white arms and petite figure.

"The dress suits you well."

"Ha-ha, thanks! You're looking good, too, Gil."

For just a moment, he opened his eyes a little wider in surprise at the compliment; he even smiled gently. Gilbert soon turned his gaze back to the door in front of them, however, and his expression became serious again.

"Are you sure you want to go inside? Janis will no doubt recognize you."

"There's no way around it. Only I can hold him back here."

Going by what Janis had told them about how his ability worked, he could only bring out Obstructions in people whose seeds hadn't yet sprouted. Which meant that Cecilia, whose seed blossomed into the mark of a Holy Maiden candidate, and Zwei, whose seed Janis had already germinated once before, were immune to him. They needed to have at least one person on each team who might come into contact with him. Plus, Cecilia could erase any Obstructions he managed to call forth.

Cecilia straightened her posture and looked up at the door. Both Janis and Oscar were on the other side. She pulled Gilbert, her escort, closer to her.

"Don't worry. I'll keep you safe," he whispered.

Feeling her courage surging back, she looked Gilbert in the eyes and gave him a big smile.

"And I'll be keeping YOU safe!"

Gilbert snorted in amusement before gently tugging her arm.

"Well. Shall we?"

"Let's do this!"

They opened the door at the end of the hallway. And so began the night that would decide their fates.

They were greeted by the dazzling sights of a magnificent ballroom: glittering chandeliers hanging from the ceiling, music played by an orchestra, and a stunning array of women dressed to the nines. Everyone seemed to be greatly enjoying themselves.

Cecilia spotted Oscar and Janis in the very middle of the busy room. On the surface, they appeared to be engaged in a pleasant conversation.

She and Gilbert walked inside, and a wave of surprised murmurs passed through the crowd. Feeling eyes on her, Cecilia again straightened her back. She and Gilbert headed toward the two princes.

Oscar saw her first. He opened his eyes wide for a moment as he took in the sight of Cecilia in a beautiful dress. His face lit up, and he turned toward the approaching pair, ready to introduce them to Janis. He flashed him a quick formal smile.

"Please allow me to introduce you to my friend, Gilbert Sylvie," said Oscar, gesturing toward Gilbert with an upturned hand.

Gilbert nodded at Janis. Oscar moved his hand a little to the side.

"And Cecilia Sylvie, my fiancée."

Cecilia bowed to Janis and gazed at him with a graceful smile plastered on her face. Janis' eyes widened in recognition.

"You're…"

"It is such a pleasure to make your acquaintance. I'm Cecilia, daughter of Duke and Duchess Sylvie."

She behaved with all the proper etiquette expected of a noble-woman. Gone was her natural openness and naivety, replaced by cultured mannerisms. She tilted her head slightly, making her earrings sway.

"Is something the matter?"

"No..." Janis was perplexed for the briefest of moments. Then he smiled again. "Pardon my reaction. You bear an astonishing resemblance to someone I know."

"Oh, is that so?"

"It really is quite uncanny how similar you are, but your arresting beauty outshines him."

"Thank you for your kind words, Prince Janis. I see now the rumors were true. You're as glamorous as they say."

"What a joy to hear you think so!"

They smiled at each other after the obligatory pleasantries. Janis glanced around the room and shrugged.

"It would seem a good time to ask you for a dance."

"Oh? You'd like me to give you my first dance?"

"Our expectant audience might pierce us with bemused stares if we don't, I suspect."

The lords and ladies gathered in the room couldn't hide their curiosity at Cecilia's appearance. Everyone's eyes were on her little group in the center of the crowd.

"I would rather not attract unwanted attention," Janis added, offering her his hand.

As if on cue, the orchestra started playing a lively polka. Cecilia allowed Janis to lead her to the dance floor. When they took the central spot, he put her hand on her lower back to bring her closer, and they began, Janis leading somewhat sloppily.

"What an unexpected turn of events," he said to her.

"Isn't life full of surprises?"

"Not even in my wildest dreams would I have imagined that the daughter of a duke would be attending Vleugel Academy, posing as a boy."

He kept a gentle smile on as he talked. Cecilia grinned back at him graciously. The music drowned out their conversation to anyone else who might be listening. Casual observers would assume they were having a friendly chat based on their expressions alone.

"So are you here to keep me occupied while your friends rummage in my quarters, looking for the Dirk of Destiny to steal?"

"Perhaps."

"What a clever plan. I thought I'd only stop by to give my regards to Prince Oscar since he invited me to the party on short notice and go home without causing any trouble. Though to be honest, it did cross my mind that it would be amusing to awaken an Obstruction in Oscar, but he was careful not to let me get close. He's even wearing gloves," Janis said with a chortle. "And how do you feel about becoming the sacrificial lamb? Or did you not think I would do that to you?"

"Dear me. Is that a threat?"

"It's a gentle warning. Maybe you're a little curious what it feels like to get possessed by an Obstruction, like the good-natured Cuddy Miland who suddenly made an attempt on the Machias boy's life?"

Janis pulled her closer yet, no doubt trying to frighten her. Cecilia stared at him in shock, but it wasn't because she was intimidated by him.

"Who are you?"

"Excuse me?"

"I didn't mention Cuddy trying to kill Zwei Machias when we spoke last time."

Additionally, Janis had seemed entirely disinterested in talking about that incident at their previous meeting. He hadn't even been able to remember Cuddy's name. He might have recalled or discovered the details later, but that would have contradicted what Janis told Cecilia about how he made no effort to clog his memory with information about people he didn't care about.

"You even used his full name, even though you had no idea who Cuddy was the last time."

"..."

"You're not the person I talked to before, are you?"

Cecilia asked that automatically. He could of course deny it, and that'd be the end of it. She had no proof. But the man she was dancing with didn't try to bluff his way out of it.

"If only he'd pay more attention, like I asked him," he said in a calm voice that was much lower than before. He didn't sound like Janis anymore. "I told him every detail before he went to threaten the younger twin, but unfortunately, he has no memory for information he finds boring."

"Who on earth are you...?"

Cecilia stared at him, appalled. The man impersonating Janis smiled gently at her.

"I should've asked him to tell me exactly what you two talked about that time. I even got the witch to change my eye color so I'd look exactly like him. All for nothing."

Cecilia reflexively tried to move away from him, but he pressed into her to keep her close. Then he addressed her in Janis' voice again.

"How familiar are you with the customs of Nortracha, Lady Cecilia?"

"Why do you ask?"

"Did you know, for example, that when a child is born to the royal family, they find another baby born on the same day to take in and raise alongside their own, as a Nameless? To be Nameless means to have a certain very specific role, but it also serves as a moniker, since we are not given names of our own."

Just as he finished saying that, the music stopped. They went over to stand by a wall.

"The Nameless receives the same education as the royal they share their birthday with, and they also learn how to protect them by training to become a master of disguise."

"Do you mean they're effectively—"

"Body doubles, who may be sacrificed to protect the life of their royal. Children with dark eyes are usually chosen for this role since their eye color is difficult to tell apart from purple at a distance."

Cecilia immediately thought about Janis' bodyguard, who was almost always at his side. His eyes were so dark, they were almost black.

Janis' Nameless bowed to her with exaggerated flair, as if to thank her for the dance. When he looked up again, his eyes were smugly narrowed.

"Deception and disguise aren't only your specialty, my lady."

Cecilia noticed Gilbert hurrying over to her out of the corner of her eye. When he reached her, he leaned in to whisper into her ear.

"Jade's team is back," her reported.

The anxiety in his voice made her turn to look into his eyes.

"What's wrong?"

"They didn't find it."

"He outwitted us..." Cecilia ground her teeth.

"I thought Lord Zwei would have sent it by now," Lean said, gazing through Jade's Artifact.

She and Huey were in a grove that gave them a view of the White Shrine, outlined against the starry sky. There were lights in some of the windows. Lean seemed a little worried.

"Do you reckon something might have gone amiss?"

"It was a poorly thought-out plan to begin with. It would not surprise me in the slightest if it got thwarted right at the start."

"Ever the pessimist, Lord Huey," Lean said disapprovingly.

Her handkerchief was spread out on the ground in front of her. Zwei was to transfer the Dirk of Destiny over so that it would appear on top of it, but nothing was happening.

"Doctor Mordred hasn't returned yet, either, and it's been quite a while."

"He probably got lost in the dark."

"Can you say something heartening for once?"

Mordred had gone on a short reconnaissance outside the grove fifteen or so minutes earlier. Lean and Huey had asked him not to, but he'd assured them that he wouldn't go far and would be back shortly.

"We may just as well give up on going into the shrine without him to guide us."

"Don't be so negative. I have the map he drew earlier."

Mordred had been investigating the shrine in the course of his Obstructions research since the two were closely related. He was to serve as their guide once they were inside because Grace's information alone wasn't sufficient to lead them to the innermost sanctum in an efficient manner.

"Your determination is truly commendable," Huey said sarcastically.

"Ah, so this is where you've been hiding," someone said suddenly in a calm yet pleased voice.

They turned, startled.

"Who's there?!"

It was too dark in the forest, which was thick with trees, to see who had addressed them. Their footsteps were getting closer, though, and eventually they came into view under the light of the moon…

"Prince Janis…," Lean's voice faltered.

Huey stepped in front of her to shield his girlfriend.

"How did you know!"

"The trap you set for me was blatantly obvious," Janis replied with a smug smile. He started walking toward them, his ashen cloak fluttering in the wind. "Considering our, let's say, strained relations, an out-of-the-blue invitation to a party at the palace seemed rather suspicious, you know? But it would have been rude to turn it down, so I was in a bit of a bind."

"Don't come any closer!" Huey shouted a warning and drew a knife from a sheath at his belt.

"Oh, how scary!" Janis raised his hands in a gesture of surrender. "Let's not be so rash. I have no intention to hurt you. And frankly, I doubt I would stand a chance if we were to fight anyway."

Huey just stared at him.

"You may not believe me, but I'm a pacifist. I've come to talk to you, that's all," Janis added with a disarming smile, trying to not look threatening.

"Talk about what?" asked Huey, not trusting him at all.

"Hold on a moment."

Still holding his hands up, Janis took a few steps backward and disappeared into the darkness. He soon returned, dragging something with him…

"Doctor Mordred!"

"I came across him a little while earlier and I thought I might as well try to capture him. I'm not strong by any means, but I suppose between me and him, I'm the more skilled fighter."

He was holding Mordred by the lapels of his coat. The doctor appeared to be unconscious. Janis lowered him onto the ground and crouched next to him. Then he took something out from an inner pocket and patted Mordred's cheek with it.

"Retreat and I won't kill him."

"That dagger...!"

"Oh, you recognize it? It's called the Dirk of Destiny, right? It's merely a trinket with no use to me, besides this."

It was without a shadow of a doubt the dagger of legend. Although Lean hadn't seen the real thing before, it matched the illustration Grace had shown her.

"By the way, didn't the doc research Obstructions? Wouldn't it be poetic if he were slain with the Dirk of Destiny? Talk about the culmination of his research!"

Greatly enjoying himself, Janis gently pressed the tip of the dagger against Mordred's neck. A little red droplet appeared, contrasting with the doctor's pale skin. Janis looked up at Huey and Lean with challenge in his eyes.

"Well, what's it going to be? Will you go back home, or do I have to kill him?"

Lean frowned, making a pained expression. So many things had gone wrong—Janis was here, he still had the Dirk of Destiny, and worse still, he was threatening to kill their friend with it. Their plan had failed spectacularly.

"And if we leave, you'll let him go?"

"Sure. In half a year or so."

"What?" growled Huey.

"Why would I let him go now, only for you to try to lure me out again to steal the dagger? I'd rather not have to deal with that sort of nuisance."

"You're taking him hostage?"

"Correct. Don't worry, you'll have him back as soon as I'm finished with my scheme. Honestly, I couldn't care less about Obstructions vanishing for good, but now's not the time. Would you mind putting a hold on that until I've done what I need? Then I can even send you the dagger along with Mordred." He laughed, perfectly at ease. "Rest assured I'll be a kind host to him. He'll get three meals a day, and as long as he behaves, he won't come to harm."

"..."

"How does that sound?"

Janis' softly seductive tone of voice would have been less out of place if he were asking Lean out on a date. She gritted her teeth. What choice did she have? Even if they agreed to his terms, they'd have no guarantee of Mordred's safety.

"I'm not a very patient man. You have ten more seconds to make up your mind."

"No, wai—"

"Ten... Nine... Eight..."

Janis was counting down relentlessly. Beads of cold sweat formed on Lean's brow. There was no good choice to make, and she and Huey had no means of turning this around.

I've got to think of something...

"Seeeven... Siiix... Fiiive..."

But Janis wasn't going to give her the time to think.

"Fooour... Threee..."

Lean had to make the call.

"Twooo..."

"We will—"

"Oops! My hand slipped!" Janis said with false concern in his voice, raising the dagger. He was ready to strike.

Lean realized he'd bever intended to spare Mordred to begin

with and was just toying with them. And now he was going to pierce Mordred's throat with the ceremonial dagger. Lean shut her eyes.

"Hold it!" came a voice from behind them, echoing through the wood.

Janis froze as someone who wasn't supposed to be there appeared behind the group.

"Huh? Cecilia?!"

It was her, changed back into her Cecil outfit for ease of movement. She dashed over to Janis, kicked the dagger out of his hand, and cast a protective barrier in the shape of a transparent dome around Mordred using Gilbert's Artifact. Caught off guard, Janis was slow to react. Suddenly, he saw a sword flying at him. It was Oscar's skill this time. The sword circled around Janis and pinned him by his cape to a tree. Meanwhile, Cecilia picked up the Dirk of Destiny. Janis groaned.

"Phew! Looks like we made it!"

"It wouldn't have hurt if we turned up a little earlier..."

"Regardless, it seems we saved the day."

It wasn't only Cecilia who teleported behind Lean, but Gilbert and Oscar as well. They'd all been sent over by Zwei to the location marked with Lean's handkerchief. Three people was the maximum Zwei could transport that way.

Cecilia glared at Janis, who'd sat down on the ground under the tree his cloak was pinned to.

"It's payback time, Janis!"

"Hmm, I was right. You are a fun one."

Despite the fact that he was still on the ground, Janis had regained his composure and was sneering mockingly again. Cecilia glared back at him.

"I didn't think it'd be easy to get you off my back, but oh boy,

do you keep pulling the rug out from under me! It's good that I came well-prepared."

"Oh, really?"

"I'm a very cautious man, you see."

He slipped out of his cloak and stood up. They heard a rustling nearby.

"What's that?!"

Just then, figures started appearing out from between the trees. Some appeared to be soldiers, while others were clad in religious vestments. They all stared into space vacantly, and had marks shaped like thorny vines on their wrists or faces. Cecilia's crew took a step back, intimidated by the sheer number of opponents who'd come out of nowhere. There were too many for them to take on.

"My ability has this useful extra feature, you know."

"And what's that?"

"I can give the possessed simple orders. They can't go against their deep-held beliefs, but as long as there's a thought or sentiment I can pivot off, I can use that to have them do my bidding."

Janis patted a soldier standing nearby on the shoulder. He must have come from the shrine's own garrison. Cecilia recalled that some soldiers had been assigned to guard their carriage while they were visiting.

"All of the people here are Caritade believers...but they're no sympathizers of the Maiden. For some, it's hard to feel loyalty toward a leader who only ever shows herself during special ceremonies."

Now Janis pointed at Lean.

"Look, my temporary friends. Here we have a Holy Maiden candidate and her knights. Why don't you just kill them all?"

The empty eyes of the possessed soldiers and clerics immediately focused on Cecilia's group, and as one, they started running toward them. Huey quickly hoisted Mordred onto his back. They all turned in the other direction from the incoming attackers.

"We got the dirk, so let's just go to the shrine!" Cecilia shouted.

They broke into a sprint. The plan had been to use Jade's Artifact to conceal their presence and sneak into the shrine without the nuns raising alarm, but that would have to be scrapped. They'd have to force their way in.

Rather than climb over the wall around the grounds of the shrine, they had Oscar smash a hole in it with the power of his Artifact. The noise alerted guards who were patrolling nearby, and they rushed over, shouting about a break-in. But when they saw the horde following Cecilia's group, they fell silent in shock or terror. Huey knocked them out before they had the time to make sense of the situation. Despite the fact he was carrying Mordred, he was still as swift as wind.

The door to the shrine was locked, so they knocked it down. They entered the magnificent chapel. A large statue of the goddess seemed to be staring at them, standing against the background of a wall with the myth written on it. In between the pillars to the left and right were flags bearing religious symbols. Moonlight illuminated the chapel, colored by the stained glass windows.

The shrine complex was divided into three areas. The first area comprised the chapel where the resident high-ranking clerics and nuns gave their daily prayers. The central area was the living quarters of the Holy Maiden and her nuns. Lastly, there was the inner sanctum located in the back of the complex, which was only opened when it was time for a maiden candidate to ascend to the title Holy Maiden.

Cecilia and her friends needed to get to that sanctum. They smashed a side door and exited the chapel into a corridor leading to the nuns' quarters. They heard many voices behind them but kept running without looking back. When they made it to the central zone, they barred the door at their backs, and the voices of their pursuers became muted. Feeling temporarily safe, Cecilia squatted to catch her breath. Everyone except Huey, who had been carrying Mordred the whole time, was out of breath.

"Do you think…we could rest here for a few minutes?"

"Not sure that's a good idea," Gilbert replied tensely.

No sooner had he said that than they heard a loud thud, and the door bent a bit. Their pursuers were slamming their bodies against the entrance, trying to break through it.

"Yikes!" squeaked Cecilia.

"They're not going to give up so easily," Lean said in a calm voice.

The door bar was made of wood. It was sturdy, but would eventually break under the frenetic onslaught of the possessed horde.

"We've got to get as far away from them as possible before they break in…"

The barred door was creaking now as the pursuers kept ramming into it. Cecilia stood up and they were about to start running down the hallway when a door opened, and a nun poked her head out from behind it.

"Is someone there?"

The doors on both sides of the hallway led to the nuns' quarters, and it seemed they'd woken up one of them. She was dressed in a plain nightgown, rubbing her eyes sleepily. Another door opened up ahead.

"Who's making that racket so late?"

And another.

"Is it morning already?"

And another…

"Keep it down!"

More and more nuns were waking up. Cecilia gasped.

This is bad... I don't want to drag them into this!

Janis had ordered the possessed to attack the Holy Maiden candidate and her knights, but who was to say they wouldn't harm other people who got in the way?

"What was that noise? I'm trying to sleep here...," said another nun who'd just come out of a room next to where Cecilia was standing.

Cecilia turned to her and grabbed her by the shoulders.

"Please go back to your room and don't come out!"

"P-Prince Cecil?! What are you doing here?!" the nun exclaimed in a shrill voice.

"Prince Cecil?"

"Did somebody say Prince Cecil was here?!"

"Where is he?"

The surprised nun's shriek had now woken up almost everyone, and more nuns were leaving their quarters to check what was going on. It didn't take long for Cecilia to become surrounded by them.

"Did something happen? What brings you here?"

"Prince Cecil, it's so good to see you again!"

"Um, could everyone please go back to their rooms and lock their doors—"

"It's been too long since your last visit, Prince Cecil!"

"You look as splendid as ever!"

"When did you arrive?"

They had lots of questions, but they weren't listening to a word Cecilia said to them. All of the nuns living who lived here were crowding the hallway. This was bad. Really bad.

"H-hey! Please, listen!"

"Please return to your rooms!"

Oscar and Gilbert joined in, pleading with the nuns to go back to safety, but hardly anyone even noticed them. To make matters worse, Cecilia could swear the wooden door bar was creaking louder, barely holding out. She bit her lip. There was only one thing that might work. Her special skill.

She put her hand on the lower back of the nun closest to her and drew her close.

"Would you like me to start with you?"

"Wh-what are you saying…?"

The nun's face flushed with an emotion someone who'd sworn a vow of celibacy should have steered clear of. Cecilia gave the nun her seductive prince look, running her fingers through her hair as she spoke.

"It was my yearning to talk to you ladies which brought me back to the shrine. Your virtues and beauty have left me smitten."

"Oh, my prince…"

"Do invite me to your rooms to tell me about your goddess, educate me about the Church—you will find a willing pupil in me, voracious for knowledge. May your sweet lips guide me to the heavens."

The innuendo made the sisters exchange glances before they all squealed with embarrassed delight.

"I'd like to spend some time alone with every one of you if possible."

"I—I want nothing more!"

"You're welcome to see me any time!"

Cecilia tilted her head to the side and looked at the horny nuns with a playful smile.

"Will you then go back to your rooms like good girls and wait for me patiently until I knock on your door?"

"Y-yes!"

"I'll be waiting! No matter how late it gets, please don't forget about me!"

"Naughty girls who get tired of waiting and come out of their rooms to look for me lose their turn."

Cecilia flashed a dazzling smile at them, touching her finger to her lips. The nuns flushed a brighter shade of crimson, swooning. Then they walked back to their rooms in a hurry. Cecilia waved at them until only she and her discomfited companions were left in the hallway.

"Not sparing even the poor nuns, huh," Lean said testily.

"I didn't want to do that, honest, but there was no other way!" Cecilia replied in self-defense.

"Let's just go, before they break through that door!"

Oscar had the presence of mind to break up their quarrel, and they all ran down the hallway.

They ran out of the corridor into another hallway, passing by a laundry room and various storerooms. Their advantage over the pursuers wasn't that great since the nuns had held them up for so long, and they were fairly exhausted from sprinting. Huey, carrying the still-unconscious Mordred on his back, shouted something to Cecilia:

"Are you sure we're running in the right direction?"

"I don't know about directions, I'm just running!"

"Are you kidding me?!"

She was doing her best, given the situation. There was no time to take out Mordred's map or check Grace's notes to get their bearings. Cecilia remembered some of the instructions and was keeping an eye out for the features on the list, but for the most part, she was just running as fast as she could to get away from the Obstruction-possessed mob. They'd made it pretty far into the shrine, so her very rough idea of which way to go seemed correct so far.

"Sorry, I shouldn't have snapped at you. We're so out of luck, with the guy who knows the route out cold. How much longer are you going to sleep, Doc?!"

Huey shook Mordred from side to side. Suddenly, the doctor lifted his head off of Huey's shoulder.

"Where...where am I?"

"Inside the shrine!"

"How come...? Oh, right. I got attacked by a strange man in a cloak..."

"Yup, and that guy's got a bunch of minions chasing after us. Which way do we go, Doc?!"

Mordred seemed somewhat put out by Huey's demanding tone.

"Let's see..." He craned his neck this way and that, clinging to Huey's back. "It would appear that our current location—"

"There's no time! Please, just tell us which way to go!" Lean was starting to lose her nerve.

"Not so fast. We don't want to lead our pursuers to the sanctum altar. It's too risky," Gilbert said in a measured tone.

Oscar nodded.

"Assuming there's only one entrance, we'll end up trapped."

"In the worst-case scenario, they'll all gang up on us."

"Goodness gracious, we can't stand here all night! Time for plan B!"

Lean stopped. So did Huey. He set Mordred down on the floor.

"What are you talking about, Lean?"

"Huey and I will hold back the pursuers. Lord Cecil, you go on ahead with the others."

"What? You can't—"

"We can handle this, I assure you. I've prepared for the worst."

Lean lifted her arms. Her sleeves slid down toward her elbows, revealing a stack of shiny bracelets on each of her wrists. They were the Artifacts from Oscar, Gilbert, Mordred, Eins, Zwei, and Dante. She'd talked them all into handing them over in case of emergency such as this one. Lean had the whole gamut of special abilities at her disposal.

"We can always fall back on you-know-what. It'll be fine!"

Cecilia hesitated for a moment.

"All right, then. Good luck!"

She nodded at Lean, her eyes firm with determination.

When Cecilia and the others went out of sight, Lean exhaled deeply. She thought her last-ditch plan was solid, but she hadn't expected she would actually have to use it. Wielding the full arsenal of Artifacts in battle would be an entirely new experience. She'd tested them out before the start of this mission, but not against real targets.

She would never admit that she was anxious, though. She was too proud for that.

Lean activated Gilbert's Artifact and smiled fearlessly, in the hope that acting confident would help her overcome her misgivings.

"Well, Lord Huey. We've rehearsed for this. Let's put theory into practice."

"Mm-hmm. By the way, you can drop the act already, you know."

"Excuse me?"

Huey fixed his gaze on the door separating them from the blood-thirsty horde of the possessed.

"Haven't you been cultivating this Little Miss Perfect persona for quite a while? You don't need to act like that in front of me. I'm ready for the real you."

Lean didn't know what to say to that. She looked at him in silence.

"I've seen through your mask, so I already know that you have a vicious streak. That you enjoy teasing people and are constantly on the lookout for the next thing to entertain you. That you're motivated solely by your own interests, that you're extremely proud, and that you have a short temper."

"That's quite a negative image of me you're painting," Lean said with narrowed eyes.

Huey half-turned toward her, a hint of smile playing on his lips.

"Not entirely negative. I know you care deeply about your friends."

"…"

"You don't have to hide your true self from me. I don't mind if you want to carry on as before, but don't try to play goody two-shoes to impress me…" Huey turned away from her as he finished the sentence, perhaps growing self-conscious.

Lean stood there in silence for a while, staring at his back. Then she arched her lips upward.

"I've also seen through the front you put up and know that you're actually very sensitive and shy. That you're embarrassed by your own lack of confidence, so you try to emulate Dante, your idol, despite knowing you'll never be his match."

"That's harsh…," Huey said shakily, turning around toward her again.

Lean gave him a broad smile.

"I also know that you're extremely fond of me."

Huey pressed his lips together into a tight line, but he didn't deny it. There was no point in lying.

"I have indeed been treating you with reserve, showing you only the qualities I wanted you to see in me. I guess it'll be less mental work for me not to have to do it anymore."

Lean summoned Oscar's sword and sent it flying toward Huey. It traced a high arc in the air before he jumped up to catch it. He took a few swings to get a feel for it. With this blade at his disposal, he would be able to banish Obstructions, despite not being a knight. Lean and company had already established that this would work through previous hostile encounters.

Lean took a knife out of her pocket and made lots of copies of it.

"Well, Huey. It's time for a show of strength!"

"We'll make short work of that rude prince."

They smiled at each other. A fraction of a second later, the horde broke through the entrance.

"The altar should be behind this door!"

Mordred had led Cecilia, Oscar, and Gilbert into the depths of the shrine, and they were now standing in front of the room they'd been seeking. They went inside, leaving Mordred by the entrance to act as a lookout.

Inside the chamber was a statue of the goddess, identical to the one from the room where the Dirk of Destiny had been kept. The statue was holding a jug, from which water spilled out into a large marble bowl below, draining out of the hole in the middle. In front of the statue stood a long, marble table with a narrow slit in the middle. Its ornate design suggested this was where you were meant to plunge the Dirk of Destiny.

But Cecilia and her two friends weren't the only people in the chamber. There was another person there, standing with her back to them. She was of short stature and wore her red hair done up in a braid. She slowly turned toward them, and they saw a familiar bespectacled face. Cecilia gasped.

"Elza…"

"I've been waiting for you, Lord Cecil."

"It was you who swiped the Dirk of Destiny right before we found it, wasn't it?" Cecilia asked sadly.

Elza simply grinned in reply.

Cecilia had figured out who the culprit was just before the landslide, when she and Lean were conversing about how Janis managed to get into the shrine to steal the dagger. At first, Lean suggested he had been entering the shrine wearing a nun's habit for disguise, until he located the dagger and made away with it, but Cecilia dismissed that as implausible on the grounds that the shrine's security was too tight for that.

"But Janis did get in somehow! How did he do it then? Did he disguise himself as someone from the shrine?"

Lean's annoyed voice played back in Cecilia's head. It would have been impossible for Janis to sneak into the shrine multiple times without anyone noticing, but it was a fact that he'd stolen the Dirk of Destiny. They'd found his earring planted in the room where the dirk had been. Then it dawned on Cecilia: he had an accomplice at the shrine.

"When you came into my room to take a look at the broken shower, you went through my things too, didn't you? And you found the instructions on how to find the Dirk of Destiny."

"Let me check your shower. Please wait outside."

At the time Cecilia thought nothing of it, but Elza had sure taken her time inspecting the shower, and there wasn't really a need to keep Cecilia waiting outside the room for that. Only later did she realize that Elza hadn't been checking the shower but Cecilia's belongings, which included the guide to the Dirk of Destiny. That was how the cleric managed to find the dirk before Lean and Cecilia did.

"Let me guess—the ghost haunting the shrine was you, wasn't it? You'd been searching for the hidden Dirk of Destiny by night, on Janis' orders."

"Yes, that was me. I didn't start the rumors, but they worked to my advantage. They kept more nuns in their rooms at night, so it was easier for me to get around unseen."

"Was our invitation to stay at the shrine something to do with you too?"

"Indeed. It would have taken me an eternity to find the dirk searching at random, but it occurred to me you might have some information that would help me. It was just a faint hope, but I really did strike gold."

Cecilia regretted having left the map in her room, but how could she have known that the friendly cleric would turn out to be working for the enemy? It bugged her to no end.

"Why would you do that, Elza? Are you being influenced by an Obstruction, too?!"

"Now that's a silly suggestion. Holy Maidens are immune to Obstructions."

"Wait, what?"

"Oh? You didn't figure that out yet?"

Elza smiled, and then she covered her face with her hands. In the blink of an eye, she transformed from a cute young girl into a tall, beautiful woman with long hair.

"It's the first time you've see me like this, I believe."

She flashed Cecilia an enchanting smile, gathering her hair up to move it behind her ears. Even though she was the same person they'd been talking to just now, her appearance, demeanor, and even her way of talking were completely different.

"My real name is Margrit Aubry, and I am the head of the Church of Caritade, the symbol of the goddess herself. I am the Holy Maiden."

On her wrists were seven golden bracelets, their designs different from the ones Cecilia was familiar with. One of them must have granted her the ability to alter her appearance.

Cecilia was in shock. Her voice quivered as she addressed the Holy Maiden.

"B-but what about that time we met you together with Elza?"

"What you saw then was a doll, not me. I was impersonating Elza. She used to be such a good assistant to me. Unfortunately, she passed away several months ago." Margrit looked down with genuine sadness. "She was a kind person of pure heart. I can't quite wrap my head around how she could take her own life. Yet that tragedy gave me freedom."

"Have you been impersonating her ever since she died?"

"Yes. I met Janis shortly after that. He must have tried to awaken an Obstruction within me, and when it didn't work, he realized who I was."

Cecilia remembered that the nuns visiting Cigogne Orphanage told her how Elza had changed several months earlier. They attributed her newly found joy in life to the effect of Madame Neal's fiction...but that was probably when the real Elza died and Margrit took her place.

"But why are you doing all this?"

"I don't feel like explaining myself to someone I barely know. Suffice it to say, I was desperate for freedom, and I craved vengeance against the Church, which has imprisoned me here for decades."

She extended her right arm to the side, and one of her bracelets shone briefly. Three distortions appeared in the air in front of her. She thrust her hands into them.

"Did you know that your Artifacts and my Artifacts have different abilities? I wonder if you can do this."

She pulled her hands out of the shimmering distortions.

"Why, hello there."

Out of one of the portals stepped Janis, and out of another, the man who called himself Nameless. He was no longer in the disguise he'd used at the evening party at the palace. As for the third distortion...

"Crap!"

Dozens of Obstruction-possessed poured out of it. Nameless stood in front of Janis to keep him safe. The prince smiled, as if he found all of this amusing.

"Shall we start round two?"

Janis raised his hand. At this signal, the empty-eyed possessed charged at Cecilia and her friends.

"Stand back, Cecilia! Oscar!"

"On it!"

Gilbert pulled Cecilia back and Oscar leaped forward, felling three of the oncoming attackers with a single slash of his blade.

"Oh, wow. So one of them acts as your shield while the other is the sword." Janis clapped with a mockingly appreciative smirk on his face. He was paying little attention to Oscar and Gilbert—his eyes were fixed on Cecilia. "Tino told me that you're actually a girl, despite appearances."

Cecilia gathered he was referring to his Nameless. So he did have a moniker after all. Tino promptly attacked Oscar, perhaps having been previously instructed to do so by Janis. As you'd expect of the

Nortracha prince's bodyguard, he was a skilled swordsman, and Oscar was struggling to fend him off.

Janis glanced very briefly at Tino before turning his gaze back to Cecilia.

"I'm guessing you're a Holy Maiden candidate."

"So what if I am?"

"Nothing. You're of little consequence anyway."

"Oh yeah?" Cecilia's voice became lower, tinged with anger.

"You're a nuisance I could do without, but you have no power to influence what happens here. Sure, you can use that dagger, but darling, you have no Artifacts. You're just a helpless girl, and no threat to me."

She understood it was a taunt. Gilbert's Artifact would protect her from physical attacks as long as she was within its effect range, so the prince was trying to provoke her to lure her out of the safe zone.

Janis was holding a rapier. Cecilia hadn't even noticed when he pulled it out. He was always saying that he wasn't strong, that he wasn't much of a fighter, but he'd somehow knocked Mordred out with ease, so his claims could have very well been lies. She needed to be on her guard...

I know that, but...

"How ineffectual you are. You've got your dear friends fighting on your behalf like you're some kind of princess, just so you can stand back and watch them die."

"You know nothing about me!"

Cecilia crouched down and lunged at Janis. Gilbert screamed her name in panic, but she didn't look back. She attempted to attack Janis with the Dirk of Destiny...but he easily parried her strike with his rapier.

"Ha-ha-ha! You're a fool! That's all there is to know!"

Cecilia smiled.

"Are you sure that *I'm* the fool?"

"What?"

Suddenly, Janis didn't seem so sure of himself. Cecilia jumped over his attack and steadied herself, putting one hand on the floor. She stood up slowly and slashed at him again. Their blades locked. Cecilia smiled dauntlessly, her face inches from Janis'.

"Guess what, Janis. There are three Holy Maiden candidates, not two."

"What? There's another?!"

"Grace!"

That was their cue. Grace materialized out of thin air. In her hand was the Dirk of Destiny, and on her wrist—Jade's Artifact. She was right in front of the altar.

This is what Lean meant when she said they had another plan to fall back on. Grace had been on the shrine team together with Lean, Mordred, and Huey, but she was to stay invisible with the help of Jade's Artifact unless they called her. She was the ace up their sleeve, and Janis, Margrit, and Tino could do nothing to stop her at this point.

"Here goes!"

Grace raised the dirk above her head and brought it down on the altar, where it slotted easily into place.

Cecilia was expecting the altar to light up, or the shrine to begin shaking, or something else to happen in response to the Dirk of Destiny, but there was no flashy signal like that to show them it was working. The water merely stopped flowing out of the jug in the hands of the goddess statue, and the bowl underneath it soon emptied.

Janis was still stunned.

"Why...why is there a second Dirk of Destiny?"

"Simple. The one I'm using is a replica," Cecilia said matter-of-factly.

While they were running down the shrine hallways, Lean had copied the dagger. She'd given the replica to Cecilia and the original to Grace, who was following them while invisible.

Something's not right...

Still keeping her eyes on Janis, who seemed out of it, Cecilia noticed something very concerning. The water had stopped flowing after Grace stuck the dagger in the altar, which was surely a sign that they'd done everything right, but...

Why haven't the Obstructions disappeared?

The empty-eyed possessed were still coming at them, moving like zombies. Gilbert was doing a stellar job of holding them back, and Oscar was exorcising them while he continued fighting Tino, so they hadn't yet made it to where Cecilia and Janis were standing. But Margrit kept summoning more and more of them out of new portals, so their numbers seemed to be increasing overall. Janis was still in a daze, but this fact wasn't lost on him. He lifted his head up.

"Ah. So that's how it works," he muttered to himself. Then he smiled, pleased. "That's how it makes Obstructions disappear."

"You figured something out?"

"Yes—that we both made an incorrect assumption. What the Dirk of Destiny does is stop the seeds of Obstructions from being released into the world."

Cecilia stared at him blankly. Janis narrowed his eyes and explained:

"Until now, I didn't know how the Church was planting the seeds in people. It must have been through this water."

"What?"

"The water coming out of the statue was the source of the seeds. It probably flowed into the river where everyone gets their drinking water. That's how everyone in the country became contaminated with this curse."

Janis shuddered suddenly. He wasn't looking well—his face was very pale, and his brow was covered in cold sweat. Maybe he had driven himself to exhaustion by using too much of his power. Tino moved to the prince's side to support him in case he fell. Janis' health must have been more of a concern to him at that moment than keeping Oscar occupied.

Despite how frail he looked as he leaned on Tino, Janis kept smiling.

"The seeds which have already been planted will continue sprouting into Obstructions until the next Holy Maiden is chosen. Meaning that every last one of your citizens will eventually become possessed if someone kills all the candidates."

"..."

"Pity that I'm too tired to take care of that right now. Let's call it a day."

Janis' breathing became labored. With effort, he took a deep breath and then turned away from Cecilia.

"Tino, Margrit, we're leaving. I need a break."

They both acknowledged his order and Margrit opened another portal for them.

"Bye, Cecil. Let's meet again, if you're still alive by then," Janis waved at Cecilia just before the portal closed.

At the same time Janis' party disappeared, one last portal left behind by Margrit ejected another large group of possessed into the room before it also shut.

Gilbert, Oscar, Cecilia, and Grace were on their last legs. They stood in a small circle, facing outward.

"It's not looking good."

"Indeed."

"Neither Cecil nor I are adequately equipped to fight them. Prince Janis rightly noted how helpless we are without Artifacts."

"I'm so sorry, everyone. I wouldn't have got you involved if I knew how dangerous it would turn out to be, Grace…"

Cecilia bowed low in a sincere apology. Grace smiled, a little nonplussed.

"Why wouldn't I help you out, considering what we have in common?"

"Sorry to interrupt, but we should talk about how we're going to get out of this. How much longer will the dome hold out, Gilbert?"

Oscar was referring to the transparent protective field Gilbert had created around them using his Artifact. Gilbert thought for a moment.

"It wears out when I wear out… About thirty minutes, I reckon."

"Right. So we have half an hour to think about how we're going to deal with the possessed and make our escape from the shrine."

"It's probably too optimistic to hope Lean and Huey will be free to join us in time."

Thirty minutes wasn't long, and they couldn't afford to spend that whole time making a plan only to have to face the enemy without Gilbert's shield abilities.

I've got to come up with something fast…

But their opponents were far too numerous to bring down in half an hour. If they all could fight, maybe they would be able to pull that off, but it would be only Oscar and Gilbert versus the entire horde.

Could we sneak out of the room using Jade's Artifact?

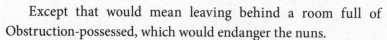

Except that would mean leaving behind a room full of Obstruction-possessed, which would endanger the nuns.

There's got to be a way, though, right? Right?

Just as the fact that they were in a hopeless position began to sink in, the door to the altar room slammed open. The possessed who were nearest to it began to tumble down to the ground, and soon a familiar face came into view.

"Tsk-tsk. You're up to your neck in trouble again, I see."

"Marlin!"

Another face popped up from behind her.

"The true hero is always late to the party, am I right?"

"Dante!" Oscar shouted in relief.

He must have gotten in touch with Marlin and asked her and her crew to come along. Behind them were also Lean and Huey, looking fairly worn out, and Mordred, his clothes in tatters for some reason. He must have also been through quite the ordeal.

Marlin smiled wider and gave an order:

"It's your time to shine, guys! Round up each and every one of these troublemakers!"

A week had passed since the showdown at the shrine.

Back at the academy, Cecilia was spacing out on a bench in the courtyard. Few students stayed on campus during the winter break, so she had the courtyard all to herself.

She sighed, idly gazing at the slate-gray sky. It had been a busy week for her. First, the king had found out about her cross-dressing.

"What on earth were you doing, Cecilia?"
"Your Majesty, it's...it's complicated..."

The mysterious Cecil Admina had been involved in so many odd incidents that eventually, the king took notice and had him investigated. Despite Cecilia's and her allies' best attempts, they couldn't stop him from discovering Cecil's true identity.

Yet the king was more interested in the fact that Cecilia's group of friends had exorcised an eyebrow-rising number of Obstructions, rather than her attending Vleugel Academy under a false name. He'd actually let the matter of cross-dressing slide for the time being. Though he didn't have much of a choice...

* * *

"Your Majesty, I would like my daughter to keep dressing as a boy at the academy."

Cecilia's mother, Lucinda Sylvie, who had also been summoned to explain the situation, informed the king cheerfully of her intentions. The king had been visibly taken aback, but she would not relent.

"You would surely not want to damage my daughter's reputation by allowing rumors about her dressing as a boy to spread?"
"It's not a rumor, it's fact—"
"Let's not forget that she's your son's fiancée. Such tales might lead to unpleasant gossip about your own son's...proclivities."

Lucinda would threaten even the king for the sake of her beloved daughter. She could be very intimidating in her overprotective mode. She and the king were close friends, but their relationship dynamics were such that the king was more like a hapless younger brother, and Lucinda like his domineering older sister.

The king shuddered at Lucinda's glamorous but well-meaning smile.

Consequently, Cecilia was in her Cecil outfit as usual.
"Mom was right. I can't just start turning up for classes as Cecilia all of a sudden."
Everyone would instantly recognize her as their Prince Cecil. Even if she let her hair down and stopped binding her breasts, her face would be exactly the same, so she wouldn't be fooling anyone.
And that's not the only problem right now...
"So that's where you were hiding!"

Cecilia turned in the direction of the cheerful voice. Lean ran over to her and tugged at her arm, pouting.

"What are you doing here anyway? We've got to prepare for the party!"

"Oh, right!"

"Don't tell me you forgot about it! You're really out of it…"

It was the thirty-first of December, the last day of the year. Cecilia and her friends were going to have a New Year's party together. It wouldn't be just the students—Grace and Mordred were coming as well. Oscar said he'd be able to join at some point, too. Gilbert had been making various arrangements to prepare for the gathering since the day before. Eins and Zwei had gotten a care package from their parents and were going to bring the food to the party. Jade, Dante, and Huey also said they were preparing a fun surprise.

Lean shook Cecilia's arm, looking a bit peeved.

"You can't just sit here avoiding everyone, Miss Holy Maiden."

"Ugh…"

Cecilia brought her hand to her chest dramatically as if she was having a heart attack. That was the other problem she'd been agonizing over. It had been all but decided that she would be assuming the role of the next Holy Maiden. She was already being treated as the provisional Holy Maiden, with Gilbert as her provisional Holy Knight. She was on track to become both the queen of the nation and the head of the Church of Caritade, which sounded like way too much responsibility to her. She'd never asked for that.

"Why does it have to be me?"

"Because we returned the Artifacts?"

After the battle at the shrine, Grace and Lean returned the Artifacts they had been borrowing to their original owners. Then they reported to the king that they'd played no part in the incident, claiming it was Cecilia and the knights who exorcised the Obstructions. It would have been rather awkward for Cecilia to go up to the king now to tell him that the other two candidates had shamelessly lied to be left out of this annoying Holy Maiden business. Telling falsehoods to the king without batting an eye was far beyond Cecilia's capabilities.

"Did you miss the part where I told you becoming the Holy Maiden is a death sentence for me?!"

If Cecilia is selected to become the Holy Maiden in the game, an event happens where she gets killed in a bandit attack on her carriage. Considering everything that had transpired, the future might not exactly follow the course of the game, but the risk was still there.

Lean pointed her index finger upward.

"That's guaranteed not to happen for at least three months. Besides, we're stronger than some bunch of ragtag brigands."

"I guess that's true…"

"And after the current Holy Maiden's mischief, the very institution of Holy Maidens may end up becoming a thing of the past. Think positive!"

"R-right…"

Of course, Lean wasn't that bothered because it wasn't her life that was in danger… She had made a good point about the possibility of the Church being reformed after Margrit's evildoing, though. There already were calls to give Holy Maidens more freedom rather than force them to live like prisoners at the shrine. Old institutions were prone to resist change, but Cecilia would be a special case, a queen-Maiden. And locking up a queen would be frowned on by the people of Prosper Kingdom.

Plus, if what Janis said about the reason for Obstructions was true, then Holy Maidens would no longer be necessary, unless the

Church wanted to keep someone with that title for purely ceremonial purposes. The king had sent people out to investigate this matter.

Lean vigorously patted Cecilia on the back.

"Ouch!"

"Don't sulk so much. Life is to be enjoyed! We're lucky to have gotten a second chance, but we might not get another, so don't waste it!"

Easy for her to say, when she was free to do whatever she wanted, unlike Cecilia.

But well, sitting here moping isn't exactly going to help with anything...

Cecilia let Lean drag her off the bench, letting out a deep sigh. Her breath briefly turned into a white puff in the chilly air.

"So far I'm still alive, which is a win already."

She'd made it through spring, summer, and fall. That was over nine months already. Maybe she didn't have to worry so much anymore. Janis had slipped away and was sure to appear again someday, but they'd fought him off once. They could do it again.

"Cecil! Lean! Everyone's waiting for you!"

Jade waved to them from a distance. He must have come out to get them. Lean pulled Cecilia by her hand.

"Come on, let's go!"

"Okay!"

New threats might await Cecilia in the near future, but she decided that whatever happened, she'd probably find a way to deal with it. Her natural optimism was a blessing, but it was also her curse.

It was the evening of December 31.

"Shall we begin? Happy New Year, everyone!" Jade raised a toast.

The table in the middle of the dorm lounge was laden with all kinds of dishes. It was a more extravagant feast than even the one they had after Advent. All the usual suspects were present, including Mordred and Grace. As promised, Oscar came to join them once he was free, which brought up the number of partiers to eleven.

"It's not even close to midnight yet."

"Patience, Jade, patience."

Huey and Gilbert looked at Jade without enthusiasm.

"It's all right, he can raise another toast in a couple hours. More fun! Wouldn't you agree, Zwei?" Dante, who'd also been pretty hyped for the party, sided with Jade.

"Um, sure," Zwei replied with a shy smile.

Mordred pinched the bridge of his nose, foreseeing trouble.

"Enjoy the party, but for the love of the goddess, keep it within reason. This is an academic institution and I'm supposed to be supervising you, so if this thing starts going off the rails, I'll have to terminate it immediately—"

"Just drink with us, what's the problem!" Eins protested.

"Yeah! You got invited as a friend, not a despotic supervisor!" Dante chimed in.

Oscar tried to rein them in.

"You're putting Doctor Mordred in a difficult position. He'll be held responsible for your bad behavior, you know."

"He'll have to ring in the new year by looking for a new job." Grace was more direct.

"Please don't even joke about that." Mordred tensed up, his face going pale.

Jade, in his own little bubble, spoke up again, sentimentality in his voice.

"This was one action-packed year, wasn't it?"

"It certainly was," Zwei agreed with a wry grin.

"It kept me entertained!" came Dante's predictable reply.

"At least one of us thrives in a high-stress environment," mumbled Huey.

Eins looked across the room to where Cecilia was sitting.

"And we all know who to thank for bringing so much hustle and bustle into our lives," he said pointedly.

"Huh? Me?" Cecilia opened her eyes wide in surprise, pointing at herself.

As one, all of her friends sitting around the table nodded.

"You're really lacking self-awareness. You're a troublemaker par excellence," Oscar informed her.

"Wait, you think it was all because of me?!"

"Um, hello? Earth to Cecil?" Dante said in between bursts of laughter. "How did you miss the fact you're always at the center of every incident? Poor Gil, my sympathy goes out to you!"

"Why am I being pitied?"

"Having such a bumbling...friend who's a magnet for trouble must be severely testing your angelic patience!"

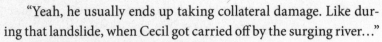

"Yeah, he usually ends up taking collateral damage. Like during that landslide, when Cecil got carried off by the surging river…"

"Gil went through hell that day, too."

Cecilia turned to Gilbert, alarmed by the twins' remarks.

"Wait, I didn't know about that!"

Gilbert grimaced, evidently not wanting to talk about it.

"We'd all been telling him to wait before going looking for you after the rain stopped, but he wouldn't listen. He yelled at us furiously to get him a carriage right away."

"Even Doctor Mordred couldn't stop him."

Lean and Jade filled her in. Dante half-closed his eyes wearily.

"Everyone was panicking, it wasn't just Gilbert. Especially after Oscar thought it a wise move to jump into the river after Cecil…"

"Eins and I couldn't believe it when we heard about it."

"He wasn't the only one with such bright ideas."

"What are you saying, Lord Huey?" Though still smiling, Lean was glaring at her boyfriend with a menacing look in her eyes. She didn't want Cecilia to know that she, too, had been desperate to save her.

"I'm so sorry for putting you through that…"

Cecilia hung her head, looking so pitiful that everyone wanted to say something to cheer her up. Dante raised his hand, and they let him speak first.

"By the way, there's something I've been wondering about for a while and this seems like a good opportunity to ask you about it."

"Sure, what is it?" Cecilia was naively not on her guard despite Dante's suspicious grin.

"You almost drowned, right? So when Oscar saved you… Did he do it?"

"Do what?"

"The kiss of life. ♡"

Gilbert gasped and shot his eyes over to Oscar. There was murder in them. Oscar quickly shook his head.

"No, I didn't."

"But how else did you resuscitate Cecil if not by mouth-to-mou—"

"Enough, Dante!"

"Oops, someone's got a short temper!" Dante giggled like a little girl.

Gilbert was still glaring at Oscar with a threatening aura, but that was just posturing. Cecilia smiled self-deprecatingly, not wanting to contribute to that conversation. She felt a tug at her sleeve and turned, meeting Lean's worried gaze.

"Is something wrong? You're being very quiet."

"I just…had something on my mind." Cecilia couldn't hide anything from her best friend. She faced forward again, staring down at the table. "I hope Margrit is okay…"

When the others mentioned the day of the landslide, Cecilia thought back to Elza—or Margrit, her real name. They'd spent only a few days together, but Cecilia really enjoyed "Elza's" company. To what extent had their time together been only an act on Margrit's part? She wanted to believe that at least some of it was genuine. It hurt too much to imagine that their brief friendship was just a lie.

Lean must have guessed what was going on in Cecilia's head. She smiled warmly and stroked her back.

"Don't worry, I'm sure she's fine. Probably having a New Year's party of her own somewhere out there."

"Yeah, I guess so…" For some reason, Cecilia felt the urge to cry.

Margrit was in a house in a small, hidden settlement. She was gazing at the moon, standing on the veranda.

"I didn't know you liked candy," came a voice from behind her.

She turned away from the moon, toward her beloved Janis.

"Not particularly."

"Really? Then why have you been carrying that around like it means something to you?"

He gestured toward her hand, which was pressed to her chest. She was holding a piece of candy in a colorful wrapper.

"Well, this one is a little special."

"What makes it so?"

"It's a gift from a friend," she said after a hesitant pause.

Margrit turned to admire the moon again, clutching the candy, holding it close to her heart.

Afterword

"Try to make the afterword sound like a radio show," was the advice a more experienced writer gave me. Still, I'm just no good at this.

Hi, it's Hiroro Akizakura. It's been a while, hasn't it? Volume 3 came out in June 2021, so it's been eight months already. For me though, that's quite a fast pace. I really worked hard this time, believe me!

So here you have *Cross-Dressing Villainess Cecilia Sylvie,* Volume 4! Yay! I wouldn't have been able to write so much if it weren't for the encouragement from you all! Thank you so much! At this rate, I might even write Volume 5! But will I? I'd love to, but I may need some more support from you, dear readers, to make it a reality!

Let's talk about Volume 4 for now. Cecilia finally faces off against the final boss! The narrative's progressed pretty far, hasn't it? Another highlight is when Cecilia and Oscar...but wait, I heard that some people like to read the afterword before diving into the story. No spoilers then! Oof, I almost ruined the very best part for you... Anyhow, writing that cave scene was really fun. It would be no exaggeration to say I wrote this entire volume just so that I could include that scene! (Okay, I am exaggerating.)

Writing this volume was a breeze since I focused on plot developments that were fun for me. I didn't have much energy left for the ending, so it's a bit all over the place, but I think that fits in with the vibe of the volume. It's all over the place, just like Cecilia! What's not to love!

Besides my editor, lots of other people contributed to the creation of this volume of Cecilia Sylvie. Thank you all! Dangmill, thank you for the wonderful illustrations! Shino Akiyama, I love your manga version of the story! Big thanks to everyone at Beans Bunko editing department, the admin staff, the editors and design staff, the publishers, and the staff at all the bookstores where my novels are on sale!

I'm immensely grateful to all of you for making it possible for me to keep writing and publishing my books! I'll keep plugging along to keep you entertained. Keep cheering me on!

Take care, and let's meet again someday!

Hiroro Akizakura

HAVE YOU BEEN TURNED ON TO LIGHT NOVELS YET?